IN SEARCH OF HOME

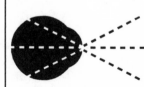 This Large Print Book carries the
Seal of Approval of N.A.V.H.

MYSTERIES OF SPARROW ISLAND®

IN SEARCH OF HOME

CHARLOTTE CARTER

THORNDIKE PRESS

A part of Gale, Cengage Learning

GALE
CENGAGE Learning™

Detroit • New York • San Francisco • New Haven, Conn • Waterville, Maine • London

GALE
CENGAGE Learning™

LIBRARY OF CONGRESS CATALOGING-IN-PUBLICATION DATA

Carter, Charlotte (Charlotte C.)
  In search of home / by Charlotte Carter.
    p. cm. — (Mysteries of Sparrow Island) (Thorndike Press large print Christian mystery)
  ISBN-13: 978-1-4104-0895-2 (alk. paper)
  ISBN-10: 1-4104-0895-7 (alk. paper)
  1. San Juan Islands (Wash.)—Fiction. 2. Ornithologists—Fiction. 3. Bird watchers—Fiction. 4. Large type books. I. Title.
PS3553.A773615 2008
813'.54—dc22   2008021746

Published in 2008 by arrangement with Guideposts a Church Corporation.

Printed in the United States of America
1 2 3 4 5 6 7 12 11 10 09 08

Special thanks to the Sparrow Island
family of authors and editors who make
storytelling a joy.

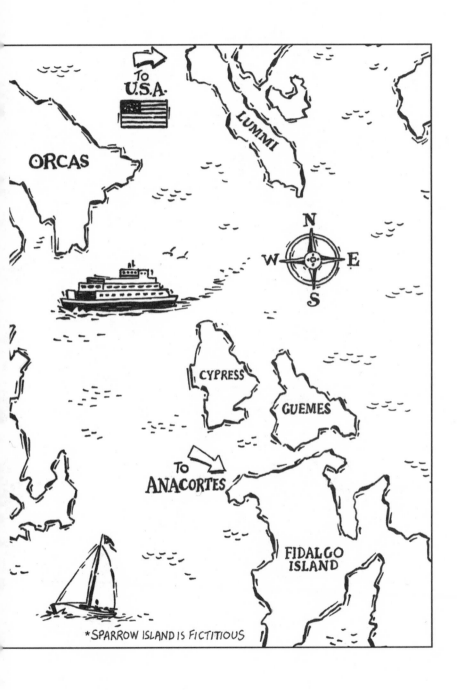

To U.S.A.

LUMMI

ORCAS

N
W E
S

CYPRESS

GUEMES

To ANACORTES

FIDALGO ISLAND

*SPARROW ISLAND IS FICTITIOUS

CHAPTER ONE

On a day like today, Abby Stanton knew she had the best job in the world.

She smiled to herself as she walked along the trail, her hiking boots flattening the grass with each step. The path followed the contour of Oyster Bay Inlet, a narrow sliver of water on the north end of Sparrow Island in the San Juan Islands of Washington State. On this early Wednesday morning in June, the sky was clear and sunny, the temperature a cool fifty degrees.

All around her were signs of God's blessings. The open forest of pines and oaks and the grassy meadow dotted with wildflowers provided a feast for her senses. The lush perfume of sea salt mixed with the scent of verdant growth. Shades of greens ranged from the bright lime of new shoots to last season's dusty pine needles. The drone of a bee as it flitted from flower to flower gathering pollen hummed in the clean air.

9

As the Associate Curator of the Sparrow Island Nature Conservatory and resident ornithologist, Abby's task today was to document the sparrow population in this part of the island. Plus, she and her friend Rick DeBow were pursuing their mutual hobby of geocaching, the international craze similar to scavenger hunting that used a GPS, a Global Positioning Satellite device. Since she and Rick had taken up the high-tech hobby, they'd found a number of the 'treasures,' which were sometimes very cleverly hidden. She hoped their luck — or skill — would hold today.

Although there was an ungraded dirt road leading to this relatively remote part of the island, they'd chosen to come by boat from the marina in Green Harbor, adding to their enjoyment of the outing.

All in all, it was a perfect way to spend a morning.

She stopped at a marker rock beside the trail and slid her small day pack off her shoulder in order to retrieve her clipboard.

"How's our position looking on your GPS?" she asked Rick.

A compact, muscular man about five foot seven, Rick was only a few years older than Abby's fifty-five years. He held an electronic device slightly larger than a cell phone in his palm. He'd downloaded topographical maps of the area from the Internet. On the device's small screen he could read their current longitude and latitude. The measurement was so precise he could identify within a few feet where they stood anywhere on earth.

Abby lifted her cap and combed her fingers through her short hair.

Today they were searching for a cache that had been listed on a geocaching Web site with clues to its specific location. There wouldn't be anything of great value in the cache — only a logbook to sign — but it felt like a treasure hunt nevertheless. Who knew what little knickknack the prior visitor might have left behind for them to find?

"Looks like we've got another couple of hundred feet to go before we reach the cache site." He looked up the hillside toward a cluster of pines, his eyes squinting in the sunlight. "That way, I think."

"Perfect. This is the beginning of the section I want to survey for sparrow population." Handing him the clipboard, she showed him a map of the triangular shaped area of land bordering the inlet. She'd drawn small circles to represent five-foot intervals. Using a shaded key, she would identify whatever sparrow activity they found.

"I hope you're not counting on me to tell one kind of sparrow from another. To me, they all look the same — little brown birds."

She laughed as he handed her back the clipboard.

"In the world of ornithology, little brown birds are officially known as LBBs, and they're ubiquitous. But don't worry about having to identify them. I should be able to handle that part of the job."

She could already hear the silver-tongued call of a song sparrow, one of the most common sparrows on the island. Scanning the low shrubs, she spotted the source of the musical notes about twenty feet from them. She pointed out the small bird sitting on a branch.

"Sometimes sparrows are hard to spot, so you have to identify them by their call. That one's singing, 'Maids! Maids! Hang up your teakettle-ettle-ettle.' That means he's a song sparrow."

"Amazing. I must've heard that call a thousand times, but I didn't know they sang lyrics too."

Laughing again, she adjusted her glasses and made a notation of the sparrow on her chart.

Rick was a fun companion on any outing. A former stockbroker, he'd given up the high-pressure life he had led in Texas to become a general handyman here on Sparrow Island, doing everything from fixing plumbing at Little Flock Church to repairing boat engines at the marina. As nearly as Abby could tell, he'd thrived in this new role and she counted herself lucky to have him as a friend.

"I need to transect this area to see what other sparrows I can turn up," she said. "I'll work my way up the hill toward where you think the cache is, if that's okay with you."

"No problem." Tucking his fingertips in the back pockets of his jeans, he appeared to take in the landscape with approval, a smile playing around the corners of his lips. "As far as I'm concerned, our geocaching expeditions are just an excuse for getting away from town and enjoying some serious fresh air and exercise. It's a great hobby."

Abby agreed. In fact, she knew that a lot of families with children had begun participating in the experience all across the country. Probably across the world. Finding the *treasure* wasn't so much the goal as enjoying each other and the adventure.

"In fact," Rick continued in a thoughtful way, "I think we ought to have a geocaching event here on the island. You know, get other geocachers together so we can get acquainted face-to-face."

"Interesting idea. We could post the event on the geocaching Web site. We might draw people from the other islands in the San Juans, maybe even from the mainland."

Rick took a sip of water from the bottle he carried on his belt. "Don't we have some sort of a festival coming up soon?"

"The Best of Sparrow Island Festival is Father's Day weekend. Mary's on the organizing committee." As a local business owner, Abby's sister was active in the community and volunteered for dozens of projects. "I'll ask her if we can set up a geocaching booth where geocachers could gather."

"We could hand out information about the hobby to people who've never heard of geocaching too."

Abby gave him a thumbs-up. "Great idea, Rick! Let's work on that."

Agreeing easily, Rick glanced across the inlet to the far shore where there were a couple of rustic summer cabins.

"Wow! Will you look at that racing boat? You don't see many of those babies up here."

Squinting, Abby watched as a sleek white

boat with a red stripe eased into the inlet and pulled up to a rickety dock across the way. Only one person was onboard, a man wearing a cap low on his forehead.

"How much horsepower in that outboard, do you think?" She strained to make out the boat's name: *Marisa.*

"Two hundred fifty at a minimum. Bet that thing really cuts through the water when you rev her up."

"It'd be fun to take a ride in a boat that powerful, but I'd hate to buy the gas for it." She also preferred a more leisurely ride on the water so she could enjoy the experience.

"There was a time when I might have wanted to own a boat like that. But no more. The slower pace of life here on Sparrow Island suits me just fine these days."

Abby smiled as Rick started up the hill toward where he thought their cache site should be, then turned her attention back to the sparrow count. She appreciated the ebb and flow of island life more now than ever, and couldn't imagine living anywhere else. Although she would never regret the many years she'd lived and worked in Ithaca, New York, at Cornell University's Lab of Ornithology, it simply felt *right* to be home again here on Sparrow Island.

Walking about ten paces along the inlet

trail, she flushed a Savannah sparrow that rose with a *tseep*. The quick flight of the bird took it into a thicket of ocean spray, its white blossoms just beginning to bud. Although various species of sparrows often shared habitats, they each had home ground that they preferred for foraging.

In the sky overhead, a young bald eagle, one that hadn't yet acquired the telltale white topknot on its head, took flight from the top of a pine tree, spreading its wings and soaring toward the inlet in search of a meal. Abby silently wished him a good hunt.

Overall, she was sure the sparrow population on the island had decreased in recent years. Development encroached on the sites where they both nested and foraged. It was one of the penalties brought on by increasing population that birds and other of God's creatures had to pay.

Leaving the trail, she methodically transected the meadow, jotting down the location on her map where sparrows took flight or announced their presence with a song.

At one point, she heard the distinctive sharp call of a fox sparrow and smiled. Fox sparrows were rare this time of year, but they were known to nest at sea level in the islands. This one had apparently lingered in the area before migrating north for the summer.

She started up the slope toward Rick. "Have you found the cache?"

"Not yet." Somewhere along the way he'd picked up a fallen tree branch and was poking the ground while he paced off the distance between two trees. When he stepped from the shade into sunlight, the streaks of gray in his brown hair glinted.

"Did they give us any hints?" When someone hid a cache, they posted the information on the geocaching Web site, often including a hint to help the searchers if they got stuck.

"Something about twin trees and a circle." He checked his GPS unit again and shook his head. "It's gotta be here somewhere."

"Maybe it's hidden within a circle that could be drawn around the two sentinel pine trees." As she walked a circumference that took her around both trees, a rabbit bolted from under a tree root and fled up the hill. Not native to the island, the European rabbit was probably introduced in the 1800s and had thrived, to the detriment of other ground animals. Fortunately, eagles had adapted their hunting preferences to keep the rabbit population somewhat under control.

"I'm not seeing any ground that's been disturbed," Rick said.

"Hmm." Lifting her gaze, she examined the bark of the tree nearest her and the drooping branches that had withered due to lack of sun as the pine grew taller. Nothing resembled a circle, so she moved around to the other side, still looking up.

Suddenly her foot caught on something. She cried out as she stumbled and nearly fell.

"You okay?" Rick hurried to her side.

"I'm fine. I just tripped —" Then she saw it. Right beside her foot was a misshapen root that formed an almost perfect circle. "I think we have a rabbit hole that's being used as a cache."

"Wow. Look at that." Rick knelt to study the hole. Carefully, he reached inside. "A very clever cacher found this hidey-hole."

Abby held her breath.

"Got it!" He pulled a plastic container from the hole, then looked up at Abby, grinning. "Eureka!"

Hunkering down beside him, Abby said, "Let's see what's inside." The container was about six inches square and two inches deep. Not the largest cache they'd ever found, but big enough to hold a logbook and maybe something else.

"Here, you open it. You discovered the cache."

"Inadvertently," she admitted. "Almost breaking my ankle hardly counts."

While she pried open the lid, Rick picked up his walking stick and stood.

"One logbook," she announced. "And a fishing lure. Gracious, someone must expect us to catch a really big fish." She handed the Day-Glo orange lure with a treble hook to Rick.

He balanced it in his palm. "I think this might come in handy next time I'm out fishing. It might even be somebody's lucky lure. Did you bring anything to exchange it for?"

"I did." From the pocket of her birding vest, which she always wore on these excursions, she retrieved a key ring with the image of a bald eagle on it.

"Perfect," Rick said as she dropped the key ring into the container.

She sat back on her haunches to leaf through the logbook. Since this cache took some effort to get to, there weren't many entries. A Canadian visitor had signed in last summer as well as a couple from Oregon. The most recent entry was a month ago by a man from Lopez Island.

"Here's the source of the lure," Abby announced. "He says the fishing was good last month near the inlet and signed his name Fish Master."

"That's probably the chat room screen name he uses on the Internet." Idly, Rick poked the branch into the rabbit hole again. "I hope his lure works as well for me as it did for him."

"You catch 'em, I'll cook 'em."

"Great. I'll —" He stopped abruptly and squatted down by the hole again. "Abby, there's something else down here."

"I hope it's not baby rabbits. I'd hate to think we frightened a mother away from her infants."

Stretching his arm, he reached deep into the hole. "No, it's metal. Not very big. And round."

Slowly, he pulled out a metal tube about six inches long and three inches in diameter. Both ends were capped.

"Another cache beneath the one we found?" Abby questioned. "That's odd."

Rick's gaze met Abby's. "Very odd. Doesn't weigh much. Think we should open it?"

Abby couldn't think of any reason not to. It could be part of the cache they'd found, an added treasure just for the fun of it. Or it could have been placed there by someone entirely different. For what reason, she couldn't imagine.

Whatever the explanation, the container piqued her curiosity. That meant the mysterious object would bug her until she knew what was inside.

"Unscrew the cap. Let's see what we've got," she said. For all she knew, it could be empty.

Rick followed her instructions, removing the cap with care. He shook out the contents onto the ground.

Without touching them, Abby studied the three documents. She recognized one as a Washington State driver's license, another as a Social Security card.

"What's that other card?" Shifting her position, she adjusted her glasses to see it better. The size of a credit card with a white background shaded in pink, it had a picture of the owner with his birth date and place of birth along with what appeared to be an official holographic stamp.

Gingerly, Rick flipped the card over. Along the top in big letters were the words GREEN CARD. Below that was a magnetic strip.

"Looks like an alien registration card to me. Otherwise known as a green card."

"Now, why would anyone stash those documents in a hole in the ground way out here?" She contemplated the name and photo on the two cards: Davor Jovanovic, age forty-two, a dark-haired man with a full mustache and a mainland Washington address. No one she recognized. The green card indicated he was from Croatia.

"These have to belong to someone who's in the country illegally," Rick said, reaching the same conclusion Abby had. "And it's a pretty good bet they're counterfeit."

Abby looked behind her as though Davor Jovanovic, whoever he was, might be lurking nearby. But no one was in sight. The only sounds that disturbed the quiet were the buzz of insects and an occasional birdcall.

She sat back up against the tree. "Do you think this is a clandestine mail drop and this Mr. Jovanovic is supposed to come here to pick up his papers?"

"Possibly," Rick agreed. "Or he's hidden the papers here until he's ready to change his identity. Something like that."

Both prospects were no doubt illegal and wouldn't culminate in anything good, thought Abby. "I think we have to take these documents to Sergeant Cobb." Henry Cobb, a good friend of both Abby and her sister Mary, supervised the Sparrow Island sheriff's substation. "He'll know what to do."

"You're right." Rick reached for the driver's license.

"Be careful how you touch everything. Whoever counterfeited the papers or stashed them here might have left fingerprints. Henry can check them. He can tell us for sure if they're fakes." Finding a tissue in her pocket, she gingerly picked up the documents one at a time and slipped them back into the tube.

Rick screwed the lid back on. "What about the rest of the cache we found? Do you think whoever put the logbook and lure here had something to do with the documents? Used them to cover up what he was really hiding in case a legitimate geocacher like us found the site?"

"Could be. Let's take that back with us too." She hated to disturb a cacher's site. But if something illegal was going on, someone needed to put a stop to it, or at least find out what crime was being committed and by whom.

"Guess that means I don't get to keep the lucky lure." Sighing, Rick dropped it back into the plastic container.

She chuckled at his discouraged sigh and retrieved her eagle key ring. "Don't worry, it's probably a counterfeit lure anyway and the fish wouldn't go for it."

He gave her a wry smile. "Whatever you say."

Before they left the site, they swept the area with a tree branch and sprinkled pine needles around so the ground wouldn't appear disturbed. If Davor or anyone else was keeping tabs on the cache, they didn't want to alert them that someone had been there.

They walked back to the spot where they'd beached the power boat. The sun was higher in the sky than it had been earlier, but somehow the day didn't seem as bright and promising as it had when Abby started out that morning.

As if a dark cloud had passed over Sparrow Island, she shivered. She was anxious to get back to town.

CHAPTER TWO

Shortly before ten o'clock, Mary Reynolds, with the help of her service dog Finnegan, wheeled herself up the ramp to the entrance of the Dorset hotel, on the east side of Green Harbor.

A car accident, when she'd tried to avoid a deer on a back road, had left her paralyzed, but had brought her unexpected blessings as well. Perhaps the greatest blessing was that her sister Abby had returned to Sparrow Island to help her after the accident and had decided to stay. Abby had given up her research position in New York and had accepted a job at the local nature conservatory. After a bit of adjustment, both Mary and Abby had found living together a perfect way to become reacquainted and strengthen their ties of sisterhood.

God does indeed work in wondrous ways! thought Mary.

Before Mary and Finnegan reached the

elegant brass doors of the hotel, a uniformed doorman wearing a crested jacket and a cap with gold braid on it, opened the doors for them.

"Good morning, Mrs. Reynolds." He touched the peak of his cap with his fingertips. "And good morning to you, too, Master Finnegan," he said with a friendly nod toward the golden/Labrador retriever mix.

"Good morning to you, Muldoon," Mary said. "You're looking very chipper this morning."

Finnegan returned the doorman's greeting with a wag of his tail. Pulling on his harness, he continued to assist Mary through the doorway, his bright blue service cape announcing to strangers that he had a job to do.

Muldoon touched his cap again. "Thank you, ma'am. You will be meeting with Mr. Gordon and the others in the library this morning."

Smiling, Mary nodded her thanks as she went inside.

The Dorset had once been owned by a wealthy railroad man. Some years ago, Keith Gordon had purchased the four-story mansion and converted it to a four star resort hotel and spa that drew a very upscale crowd of tourists and locals. The opulent ambience was both subtle and welcoming with deep Persian rugs, plush velvet-covered couches and crystal chandeliers. Wide paths of mosaic tiles in black, cream and burgundy separated various seating areas in the spacious lobby.

In the meeting this morning, Mary would be helping Keith Gordon and other merchants in town to plan the annual Best of Sparrow Island Festival, an event similar to a farmers' market where local products as well as arts and crafts would be on display. As the owner of the only florist shop in town, Island Blooms, she was a major participant in the event.

As she entered the paneled library with its extensive shelves of books, Keith Gordon stood and stepped forward to welcome her.

"Ah, good, Mary, you made it all right I see." He took her hand and held it between both of his. His genuine warmth and soft Scottish burr made him perfect for the hospitality business he'd chosen as a career.

"It's always a delight to have an excuse to visit the Dorset," she said.

"Then we will have to create more excuses so that we can have the pleasure of your company more often."

She chuckled, and felt her cheeks flush at his compliment. He was a man in his sixties

27

with a full head of white hair not unlike her own shade of silver-gray and sported a neat goatee. Keith's Old World charm could set any woman's heart aflutter, although personally, Mary admitted, she preferred Sergeant Henry Cobb's more down-to-earth style.

Artie Washburn, a young deputy sheriff in his twenties, had also stood when Mary arrived. Handsome, with the burnished good looks of his Native American heritage, he gave her a two-finger salute. "Morning, Mrs. Reynolds."

"Good morning, Artie. And to you, Ana." Mary rolled her chair to where Ana Dominguez, owner of In Stitches, a local fabric, yarn and craft store, was seated at a large mahogany table. On the table were a silver tea and coffee service and a set of delicate porcelain cups.

Ana shared a quick hug with Mary. "How's your latest sweater project going?" Ana asked.

Mary gestured for Finnegan to lie down on the floor beside her and released her grip on his harness.

"I've started the first sleeve, so it's coming right along." Mary, along with several other women on the island, knitted sweaters all year long for a project called Warm Up

America. The completed sweaters were donated to poor children who might not otherwise have anything warm to wear during chilly winter months. Some of the group also knitted baby clothes for new mothers in need.

Mary had just taken her place at the table when Donna Morgan, the blonde owner of Bayside Souvenirs came scurrying into the library.

"Good morning, all. Hope I'm not late. I had to wait for the UPS delivery guy to bring me a shipment. He's such a dear. Always makes sure I get my deliveries first thing in the morning. Of course, sometimes my suppliers are slow, but that's not Jack's fault." She gave Keith a quick hug. "Have I missed anything?"

"Not at all, my dear," Keith said, looking a bit taken aback by her impulsive gesture. "We haven't yet begun."

"Oh, good." She started to take her seat, then circled to the other side of the chair before sitting down. She giggled a little as though embarrassed by her actions. "You know what they say, 'Sit from the right and you'll never go wrong.' "

Mary suppressed a smile. The forty-year-old divorcee appeared to have a harmless superstition for almost every situation. Mary could only wonder how she kept them all straight.

Keith offered them coffee or tea and did the honors by pouring for them. Artie passed the cream and sugar down the table along with a plate of buttery cookies.

Mary bit into a cookie, delighted with the rich flavor, and ignored the twinge of guilt for indulging in a midmorning snack as she reached for a second one.

The final member of the Best of Sparrow Island committee arrived dressed for fishing rather than for dropping in at a swank hotel for a business meeting. Brenda Wilson, the owner of the Tackle Shop, strode directly to Keith and gave him a hearty handshake.

"Caught a four-pound sea bass on a jig this morning off Paradise Cove," she announced, going around the table to shake everyone's hand. "Should've seen that baby fight. Came close to tossing the hook, I'll tell you. Had to work hard to net him."

"You put him back?" Artie asked.

"You bet. The fun is in catching fish, not killing 'em."

"Maybe someone entered in the Father-Son Bass Fishing Classic will catch him again," Mary said.

The three-week-long event culminated on Father's Day at the Dorset during the Best of Sparrow Island Festival. The winners were announced and that was followed by a huge fish fry, which had become quite popular with both locals and tourists.

Brenda pulled out a chair and sat down next to Artie. "He'll be too spooked for a couple of days to hit on anything that looks like a lure. By the weekend, he ought to be hungry enough to take a chance again."

Although Mary's father had run a fishing charter service, she wasn't much into fishing. Her late husband Jacob had loved it though, so she'd often gone with him just to enjoy the scenery and his company.

After seeing to it that Brenda got a cup of coffee, which she took black, Keith brought the meeting to order.

"I've arranged for twenty canopies to be delivered for the festival," he said. "We'll set everything up on the lawn on the side of the hotel. Suppliers can display their products on the tables we'll provide."

"I've got some guys who'll demonstrate fly tying," Brenda said. "Think we can set up to demonstrate fly casting at the fountain out front?" she asked Keith.

Stroking his goatee, Keith nodded his approval. "I think that would be fine. We'll have to rope off an area to avoid having someone snagged by a back cast, but that shouldn't be a problem."

"A fishing hook caught me on the arm when I was a kid." Artie rolled up the sleeve of his uniform shirt to show them a small scar. "Hurt like crazy."

"I'll make sure my guys are careful," Brenda assured them.

"Artie, how're you doing with Native American merchandise?" Keith asked.

"I'm good. My grandfather has lined up a couple of local carvers who'll bring their stuff — small totem poles and carved images of whales and dolphins. My Aunt Wilma will bring her woven baskets and some made by other women of Lummi ancestry."

"My local wind chime supplier is all excited about showing off his merchandise," Donna said. "I've got a woman coming with her window doodads, you know those thingies you stick on a window so the sun shines through them. And I think I've got a line on a kite maker, but I looked for his phone number yesterday and couldn't find it." She gave a helpless shrug. "I know it's in my office somewhere."

Mary knew Donna's back room was so cluttered, it posed a fire hazard. However, given enough time and plenty of digging, Donna was likely to uncover the missing phone number.

Keith went around the table, asking the committee members about their plans. Mary indicated she'd have displays of wreaths made of dried flowers available as well as potted orchids raised in a friend's hothouse on the island. She also hoped to talk with Aaron Holloway of Holloway's Hardware because she was sure some of the men who frequented the store did some fancy woodworking that they'd like to sell — small inlaid boxes and decorative pieces. She also promised to talk with her mother, who volunteered one day a week at the Visitors Center. That organization would probably want to display information about the attractions in Sparrow Island.

For Ana's part in the festival, she was organizing several of her quilters who would arrange a display, and she had a woman who made beaded jewelry lined up for the show.

They talked about contacting others to participate — a local candle maker and a woman who made delicious jams and jellies from wild blackberries.

Finally, they ran out of ideas and decided to adjourn until the following week when they'd all report on their progress.

As they began to disperse, Finnegan came to his feet and stretched, ready to be of service again.

Always the gentleman, Keith stepped behind Mary's wheelchair to push her when she was ready to leave. As they reached the library door, a young man dressed in the identifying brown pants and shirt of the housekeeping staff met them. His name tag read Damani and he was carrying a tray to pick up the remains of the coffee, tea and cookies.

"Good morning, ma'am." Smiling broadly, his white teeth contrasted with the chocolate brown of his skin. "That's a fine dog you have there, ma'am."

"Thank you, Damani." Detecting a British accent, Mary asked, "Are you from England?"

"Oh no, ma'am. My home is in Belize. I and some of my mates have been hired by Mr. Gordon for the summer."

"We're glad to have them too," Keith said. "It's getting harder and harder to hire reliable staff on a temporary basis. The young people we've hired from Belize have all been hard workers."

Damani flashed another bright smile.

Vaguely, Mary recalled Belize was a small country in Central America that used to be called British Honduras, and thus had an English-speaking population.

"So you've moved to Sparrow Island permanently?" she asked.

"Oh no, ma'am. My work visa is good for only ninety days, so I must go home then. But if I do well, Mr. Gordon will hire me again next summer." He shifted the tray he carried. "Of course, I wish I could stay forever in your country, but that is not possible."

"Getting permanent resident status isn't easy," Keith explained. "Only a limited number of people from each country are allowed to immigrate — there's a quota — and preference is given to those who already have family members here."

Damani's expression sobered. "And I am not so fortunate as that, so I must be content to spend my summers here and return home to my own people in September."

"Well, I hope you enjoy your stay," Mary said.

Keith took hold of her chair again. "We won't keep you from your work any longer, Damani."

"Yes, sir." The young man gave his employer a deferential dip of his head.

As Keith pushed her through the lobby, Mary asked, "How do you find people like Damani who want to work in the States?"

"We hire a recruitment agency. They interview in several different countries like Belize and Jamaica where unemployment's high and English is spoken. The competition for jobs in the States is fierce, so we get the cream of the crop. Unfortunately, I haven't been able to find a utilities engineer, which I could use right now."

"It's a shame a young man like Damani can't stay in the country longer."

"Remember, when he goes home, the money he's earned here goes to help support his family. He'll be a local hero and his family will be better off financially for his efforts. After he works and proves himself here or somewhere else, he may be able to find a sponsor who'll help him attain permanent status in the States."

"I guess it's not easy to come to America."

"As an immigrant myself, I can assure you it's worth every bit of effort it takes. Becoming a citizen of this country was one of my proudest moments."

They reached the door, and the doorman snapped to attention, opening it for them.

"We hope to see you again soon, Mrs. Reynolds," he said. "And Master Finnegan."

"Thank you, Muldoon." She turned to thank Keith for arranging the meeting, and he took her hand.

"I'll see you next week, Mary, if not sooner." He brushed a kiss to the back of her hand, then stood back.

As Mary wheeled down the ramp toward her van, she noticed two young men planting colorful asters and stocks in a flower bed that lined the walkway. They wore tan overalls with the Dorset logo and looked as though they could be from Belize like young Damani. At the moment, they were having a subdued but intense discussion and looked up from their work as she passed by.

She smiled, and they nodded in acknowledgement, their dark eyes following her for a moment before they returned to their task.

She wondered if they were as anxious to remain in America as Damani seemed to be. So many people in developing countries around the world longed to have a better chance in life, while those born here often took the benefits for granted.

Thank You, Lord, for the life You've given me and the freedom to enjoy it in such a wonderful country.

CHAPTER THREE

The Green Harbor Marina had slips for more than a hundred boats. During summer weekends it was a busy place with boaters coming and going, both tourists and local residents finding myriad ways to enjoy activities on and around the water.

However, this Wednesday morning in early June in the marina was quiet. Most of the boats were in their slips, protected from the elements by blue canvas covers. Only a few owners were fussing with their boats or relaxing in deck chairs on the fantails.

Abby didn't feel at all relaxed as Rick motored up to the dock and cut the engine. The uneasy feeling she'd had about the hidden documents they'd found had kept her on edge during the hour-long trip back from Oyster Inlet.

Her daypack slung over her shoulder, she hopped off the boat with the mooring line in hand and wrapped it around a cleat.

Since her father had owned a charter fishing boat while she was growing up here on Sparrow Island, she was as comfortable around boats as she was on land.

"I'll wash down the boat after we see Sergeant Cobb," Rick said. "I'm anxious to hear what he has to say about our find."

"So am I. I wonder if anyone else has found something like these IDs at a cache site."

After making sure the boat was secure, Rick joined her and they walked rapidly down the weathered wooden dock. Boats rocked gently in their slips, tugging on their mooring lines like children trying to tempt a parent to come play. Sea gulls perched on the top of masts proclaimed their territorial rights. At the rustic tables in front of the sundry shop, a lone man sat enjoying a cup of coffee.

"Let's take my car," Abby suggested. "Parking can be a problem around the sheriff's substation." Her hybrid would be easier to squeeze into a parking spot than Rick's pickup.

"Fine by me."

The downtown of Green Harbor was only a few blocks wide with many of the shops that catered to tourists located on Shoreline Drive. Abby skirted that busy area to make her way to Municipal Street. One tan and green sheriff's cruiser was angle parked in front of the station. Abby found a spot for her car and got out, taking her daypack with her.

At the substation, Rick held the door open for her. Deputy Mike Bennett, a slender man in his thirties, was working behind the counter.

He smiled in recognition. "Hi, Dr. Stanton. Rick. How's it goin'?"

"We're good," Rick said. "Is Henry in?"

"Sure. Let me buzz him."

A minute later, Henry Cobb appeared from the hallway that led to the back of the building. His tan uniform shirt was carefully pressed but his green tie was loose at the collar, the top button of his shirt undone. Unlike when he was out on patrol, he wasn't wearing his utility belt or his weapon.

He greeted them warmly and invited them back to his office where he offered them chairs.

"What can I do for you two?" he asked as he sat behind his metal desk. A computer sat beside his desk and behind him was a bookcase full of books on law enforcement and thick, three-ring binders filled with government regulations.

From her daypack, Abby retrieved the

plastic container and metal tube they'd found. "We thought you ought to take a look at these." Unscrewing the cap, she slid the documents onto his desk.

"We found them when we were geocaching near Oyster Inlet," Rick said.

Cocking his head, Henry studied the contents of the tube without touching anything, then glanced at Rick. "When you were geo-what-ing?"

As succinctly as possible, Rick explained geocaching and how the Web site had led them to the cache.

"There's also a logbook in this plastic box and a fishing lure," Abby added. "We don't know if the two finds were put there by the same person or different people."

"Either of you recognize the guy in the picture or his name?"

They both shook their heads. Abby certainly couldn't recall meeting anyone by the name of Davor Jovanovic, and surely she would, given that the name was so unusual. Offhand, she couldn't name anyone who'd been born in Croatia either.

Using the eraser at the end of a pencil, Henry slid the documents closer to study them more carefully.

"Can you tell if they're counterfeit?" Abby asked.

"I can't be sure. Rounding up illegal aliens isn't part of my job description. Only when I arrest someone who doesn't seem to have the right identification does his legal status come into question." He shrugged. "Sometimes not even then. It's the feds that worry about things like illegal aliens and deporting them. I do know that more and more illegals are making their way across the Mexican border and a few sneak in via Canada. Some even arrive here by boat."

"Here? As in here on Sparrow Island?" Abby asked.

Henry's brows pulled together. "I don't recall hearing of anyone who's actually arrived illegally on any of the San Juan Islands, except a few boaters from Canada who forget to check in with Customs. Not that there couldn't have been some. I just haven't heard of it. Used to be boaters could simply report by phone that they entered US waters. That changed recently. Now they have to show up in person with a passport."

"We both thought that the license and green card were probably fake or there wouldn't be any reason to bury them," Rick said.

Leaning back in his chair, Henry ran his palm across the top of his bald head and smoothed the gray fringe around the edges.

"Your instincts are probably right," he said, "though it looks like a pretty good job of counterfeiting to me, if that's what it is. Given all the built-in security on the card, it'd take some fancy equipment and a lot of skill to reproduce a document that looks this good. I'll have to get an ICE agent — someone from Immigration and Customs Enforcement — to take a look at these. I assume you meant for me to take custody of what you found."

"Of course," Abby agreed. "Personally, I'd like to know what this is all about. I don't like the idea of some criminal using a legitimate geocaching site for an illegal activity. I don't imagine the owner of the geocaching Web site would be too happy about it either."

"Plus," Rick added, "if there's something illegal going on, an innocent person, or even a family with kids just out to have a little fun hunting for a cache, could inadvertently stumble into trouble. I'd hate to think of anyone getting hurt by whoever stashed those IDs."

So would I, thought Abby. She hadn't considered the possible danger of disrupting an illegal scheme. She thanked the good Lord she and Rick hadn't interrupted the individual in the act of hiding the metal tube. He might not like witnesses around.

"When the ICE agent shows up, he'll probably want you to take him to the spot where you found this stuff. He'll need to know about the Web site you're talking about too." Henry used a pair of tweezers to pick up the cards and put them back in the tube.

"I'll be happy to share with him whatever I know," Abby said.

"Meanwhile, I'll check out the driver's license with the Department of Motor Vehicles to see if it's legit and have my men check for fingerprints. That might give us something to go on."

Abby was pleased Henry had taken their discovery seriously, but a part of her wanted to pursue the investigation herself. After all, if someone was committing a crime here on Sparrow Island, she'd like to see him stopped.

Perhaps she could learn something of value by exploring the geocaching Web site more thoroughly herself.

But for now, she needed to get back to the Nature Museum so she could log her sparrow sightings on the computer.

After her meeting at the Dorset, Mary dropped by Island Blooms to check in, then drove home. Of all the blessings she had received since her accident, her van was among the greatest because it provided her with the independence to go where and when she wanted. Modified for her use, it had hand controls that allowed her to drive safely. She entered via a lift and locked her wheelchair into position. Finnegan especially enjoyed his secured position behind the front seats where he could watch the passing scenery through the windshield.

Mary had lived in her two-story house on Oceania Boulevard since the early days of her marriage. She and Jacob, her late husband, had raised their two children there, and she couldn't imagine living anywhere else.

Of course, since the accident her domain was limited to the first floor, which had been remodeled to make it accessible. She was content with a spacious kitchen to cook in, a craft room for her many projects and plenty of space to entertain when she was so inclined.

As she pulled into the driveway, she touched the remote to open the garage door then slowly drove inside.

She and Finnegan had barely exited the van when a gray-and-black-striped kitten with white paws came trotting into the garage, her tail raised in a salute.

"Well, hello there. Where'd you come from?"

In answer, the kitten wove her way around Mary's foot rest, rubbing her jowls against the metal and purring loudly. She looked to be about ten weeks old and not very well fed.

"You're a friendly little thing." Reaching down, Mary allowed the kitten to sniff her hand, then picked her up.

Not in the least disturbed by the presence of their feline visitor, Finnegan observed the action with quiet stoicism.

Mary stroked the kitten's soft fur. In return, the kitten kneaded her stomach and continued to purr. "She's a pretty kitty, don't you think, Finnegan?"

The dog's ears swiveled forward attentively.

"Not very old, either. I wonder if she belongs to one of our neighbors."

Mary hadn't heard about anyone adopting a new cat, but that didn't mean anything. It wasn't news that would be widely announced.

She was, however, aware that sometimes unwanted kittens were simply dumped by their owners, thinking a cat could survive on its own. While it was true there were a fair number of feral cats on Sparrow Island, survival was not a sure thing. Given the proper motivation, a bald eagle or even a large hawk could decide to make a meal of a small kitten. And until a cat learned to hunt effectively, finding its own meal wasn't easy.

If a cat did become feral, there were other problems. They often reproduced and soon every bird in the neighborhood was in danger. Mary's sister, in particular, worried about that.

With the hand that wasn't petting the kitty, Mary released Finnegan's service cape. "You're off the clock, boy."

He shook himself but didn't seem eager to leave her side, instead keeping a wary eye on the kitty.

"It's okay. This little kitten isn't a threat to you or to our Blossom." It was true that Finnegan was particularly protective of Mary's white Persian cat, and Mary wasn't sure Blossom would be all that thrilled to have another cat in the house. A better choice would be to find the kitten's rightful owner.

At the sound of running feet, Mary turned to see her ten-year-old neighbor, Bobby McDonald, racing across the lawn from his house.

"Hi, Mary. Dad and I went fishin' today." Wearing sneakers, he slid to a stop next to her wheelchair. "Did you get a new kitten?"

"No, she just wandered over here. Do you know where she belongs?"

"Nope. Can I hold her?"

For once, Bobby's attention was diverted from Finnegan, whose tail was wagging like crazy.

"Of course you may. But why don't you say hello to Finnegan first, so he won't get jealous. Then you can hold the kitty."

"Oh sure." With plenty of enthusiasm, Bobby ruffled Finnegan's fur and gave him a big hug before easing the kitten from Mary's lap.

"Does she have a name?"

"I have no idea."

Bobby cuddled the cat up to his face. A day in the sun had emphasized the smattering of freckles across his nose. "She's cute. Her fur's so soft and she's so little."

"Smaller than she should be," Mary agreed. She had the troubling feeling the kitten had been dumped by a thoughtless owner.

"Maybe tomorrow you can check around the neighborhood to see if she belongs somewhere."

"Sure, I can do that."

During this first week that school was out for summer vacation, children latched onto any activity to keep themselves busy, thought Mary. Fortunately, Bobby was a very bright young man and could most often entertain himself.

From the adjoining yard, Neil McDonald made his way toward Mary and his son. Wearing jeans and a flannel shirt, he looked like a lumberjack rather than the seaman that he was, manning the ferries that carried freight and people between the mainland and the San Juan Islands.

"Hope my boy isn't bothering you," Neil said as he joined them.

"Not at all. He tells me you two went fishing today."

"Got totally skunked, I'm afraid. Not even a nibble." With his big, callused hand, Neil gently stroked the top of the kitten's head. "We're out to win the Father-Son Bass Fishing Classic, but we sure didn't have much luck today."

"I was talking to Brenda Wilson this very morning," Mary said. "Brenda hooked a four-pound bass off Paradise Cove."

Neil's eyes widened. "Did she catch and release?"

"That's what she said."

Abruptly, Bobby dropped the kitten back

into Mary's lap. "Can we go there next, Dad? Maybe we could catch him and win the trophy."

Cupping the back of the boy's head, Neil smiled down at his son. "My next day off, I promise."

"Ah, gee, if we could go tomorrow . . ."

"Don't you worry, Bobby. Brenda said the bass would be spooked for a couple of days so maybe he'll be really hungry when you go fishing again with your father."

Bobby appeared reasonably mollified by that possibility.

"So what are you doing with a new cat?" Neil asked.

"I'm afraid she's a stray," Mary admitted. "Bobby's going to check around the neighborhood tomorrow, see if he can find the owner."

"Good idea." Neil hooked his arm around his son's shoulders. "Mom says she's got some chores for us. You ready to go home?"

A suspicious frown furrowed the boy's forehead. "What kind of chores?"

"I think it has something to do with lemonade and chocolate wonder cake. But if you don't want to —"

"Cool!" Bobby shot off toward home like he was a Fourth of July sky rocket.

Neil chuckled. "If only we could get him

to clean his room that fast, Sandy would be in seventh heaven."

Mary completely understood. Her son Zack hadn't been all that enthused about keeping his room neat at that age. Fortunately, he'd grown into a fine man and was a talented keyboard player with his own musical group. Mary's only regret was that his travels meant she didn't get to see him as often as she would have liked.

By now, the kitten had stopped purring and had curled up into a tight ball on Mary's lap and fallen fast asleep. She was reluctant to dump the poor little thing out of her lap, not when she knew the kitten was probably hungry. She also didn't want to leave the kitty outside overnight. Not without a home to go to.

Admitting she was a sucker for almost any needy animal and was equally skilled at rationalizing her actions, she kept the kitty in her lap as she wheeled herself into the house. With any luck, the kitten would only be here for one night.

Tomorrow Bobby would locate the owner and she'd be able to reunite the young tabby with her real home.

CHAPTER FOUR

The sun was casting long shadows and the afternoon air had grown cool by the time Abby left the Nature Museum for home. In spite of keeping busy with data entry and research regarding grant applications, her thoughts had often drifted back to the documents she and Rick had found and what they might mean.

When she arrived home, Mary was in the kitchen starting dinner, rolling chicken breasts in crushed french fried onions before baking them.

"I'm home," Abby said.

"I was just getting ready to —"

Before Mary could finish her sentence, a small inquisitive kitty jumped up onto the counter to investigate what was going on.

"Oh no, you don't!" Mary tried to snare the kitty, but the kitten scampered out of reach onto the window sill behind the sink, apparently intrigued by the bright Rhode

Island Red rooster pattern on the curtains.

With a quick lunge, Abby snatched up the kitty. "My, my. Do we have a new member of the household?"

The sudden activity caused Finnegan, who'd been lying on the floor near the kitchen table, to come to his feet ready to assist in any way he could.

"Oh dear, I hope not." Mary wiped her hands on a paper towel. "She's about more than I can handle."

The kitten batted at Abby's hair. "Where'd she come from?" Chuckling, Abby snared the animal's snowy-white paw. "My goodness but you're feisty."

"I think she's a stray, but Bobby's going to check with the neighbors tomorrow to see if she belongs somewhere nearby. I didn't want to leave the poor little thing outside. The nights are too cold for a baby like her."

"And here I thought I was the only one who was softhearted around here." Amused, Abby unstuck one of the kitten's claws from her blouse and placed the little ball of fur on the floor.

The kitten scampered right up to Finnegan, hunched her back and hissed.

More surprised than afraid, Finnegan took a step back. He looked up at Mary as though asking for an explanation for the cat's misbehavior.

Abby laughed. "What a brave little homeless kitty. Poor Finnegan."

"A naughty kitty, I'd say."

The creature in question, having gotten her way with the dog, trotted over to Blossom's dish and began to snack on the crunchies.

"What does Blossom think of our visitor?" Abby asked.

"Not much. I'm afraid she's gone into hiding."

"Smart cat."

The kitten lost interest in the food, tried to jump onto a chair, overshot her mark and tumbled off on the other side. Landing on her feet, she raced into the dining room.

Chuckling, Abby said, "I have to go wash up and change. Would you like me to take the kitty upstairs to get her out of your hair while you finish fixing the chicken?"

"Bless you, sister. That little creature, dear as she may be and as full of spunk, can be a real pest."

"Okay, little Miss Mischief can come upstairs with me and we'll see what sort of trouble she can get into there. Assuming I can catch her, that is."

"I'm afraid Mischief is an all too apt name

for her," Mary said.

Abby soon discovered the best method of getting Miss Mischief to do anything was to use a long string as bait. The kitten bounded right up the stairs behind her in pursuit of the lure.

Once in her bedroom, Abby stopped pulling the string. Miss Mischief tackled the end of it, rolling the string and herself up like a ball of twine.

"You're just full of it, little lady." Laughing, Abby imagined the havoc Miss Mischief would make of Mary's knitting yarn and closed the bedroom door in order to keep the kitten safely confined. For the moment.

Stepping into the closet, Abby picked out a pair of slacks and a clean blouse to change into. While her back was turned she heard the telltale *clink* of porcelain on porcelain.

Hastily, she stepped back into the bedroom. "What are you up to?"

While exploring the top of Abby's dresser, the curious cat had knocked over one of Abby's porcelain birds. She had a small collection, most of them gifts from friends.

"Oh no, you don't!" She scooped up the kitten, righted the red-breasted robin that had been knocked over, and dropped Miss Mischief to the floor.

Undaunted, the kitty leaped back up to

the top of the dresser only to be snared by Abby, who reacted quickly before Miss Mischief could do any damage.

"Whatever are we going to do with you?" This time she plopped the kitten in the middle of her double bed, right on top of the colorful handmade quilt Mary had given Abby. After a few exploratory circles around the bed, Miss Mischief finally settled down and began to bathe herself.

Abby exhaled in relief.

A few minutes later, changed into clean clothes, Abby went downstairs to the kitchen again.

Mary looked around warily. "Where's that little mischief maker?"

"Sound asleep in the middle of my bed."

"Thank goodness. What a handful she can be." Mary wheeled herself to the stove. "I put on the tea kettle. Will you have a cup?"

"Perfect. Just what I need after a day like today."

Mary lifted her brows. "That bad?"

"No, not bad, but definitely interesting." While they waited for the tea to steep, Abby told her sister what she and Rick had found at the geocaching site.

"I didn't realize we had an illegal alien problem here in the islands," Mary said as she poured the tea.

"Henry doesn't really think we do. But he does suspect the documents are counterfeit and so do I."

"Does he think what you found is related to some . . ." — Mary paused — "something related to terrorism?"

"He didn't say." And Abby hadn't actually considered that, though it could be possible.

"I met this really nice young man from Belize at the Dorset this morning. He's here working at the hotel for the summer. Certainly, he seemed enamored of the idea of staying in the States permanently, but I don't think he'd do anything illegal to make that happen."

Slowly, Abby sipped her tea, a nice herbal blend. "I imagine there are a lot of reasons why someone would pay to have a forged green card so they could stay here indefinitely. But there could well be other, more nefarious reasons too."

"Like terrorists?"

"Yes. But also people who might be fleeing a violent dictatorship. Or a run-of-the-mill criminal who's looking for a new home for his schemes. Or the suspect might simply be creating a new identity to hide from someone else."

Mary set her cup down heavily. "So this person whose identity papers you found could be an innocent victim simply trying to escape detection by some criminal element?"

Abby shook her head. "I don't know. Hopefully, we'll know more after Henry contacts the Immigration and Customs officials. For now, everything's supposition." Abby didn't like guesswork. She needed facts. That's what her science background had taught her.

At the moment, all she knew was that she and Rick had uncovered some suspect documents that might — or might not — be counterfeit. In either case, the reasons the documents had been hidden in a hole were not known.

And that was what made her curious.

"Oh, I almost forgot about Rick's idea," Abby said. "We'd like to organize a geocaching event at the festival, if there's room. You know, provide a place for geocachers to say hello to one another."

"I think we can do that. I'll pass on your request to Keith Gordon. He's providing all the facilities. At the very least, you geocachers can share space with the Visitors Center. I'm hoping Mother will help out with that."

After dinner, Abby chatted awhile with Mary, then went upstairs to use her computer. She wanted to check the geocaching Web site to glean any clues about who planted the false documents and why.

She noted Miss Mischief was no longer napping on her bed. Listening a moment, she couldn't detect any sound that suggested the little kitty was getting into trouble again, so she sat down at her desk and booted up her laptop.

Normally, after locating a cache, she'd log her success, make some comment of thanks for the fishing lure and move on to something else. This time, she didn't want whoever had planted the presumably false documents to know she and Rick had been there.

She did scroll back through previous logs, however, and found Fish Master's notation. He appeared totally legitimate, a regular geocacher who'd uncovered any number of caches and was proud of it. She doubted that he'd planted the documents or knew anything about them. Although, since everyone used screen names — in effect aliases — it would be interesting to discover the Fish Master's real identity.

Paging back to the home page, she entered the ZIP code for the San Juan Islands and proceeded to check other caches that had been listed in the area. Fish Master had visited several; obviously he was a resident, as he'd indicated in the log. Beyond that, she had trouble determining any pattern that might lead her to whomever had hidden the IDs.

She'd just checked into the forum section where members made comments when she heard Mary yelling from downstairs.

"Abby! I need you!"

In a flash, Abby was out of her bedroom and running down the stairs. She'd left Mary watching a PBS show on television about Amish quilting. Now she found her sister staring up at the top of the curtain rod across the living room window. Finnegan was gazing upwards as well.

And there, balanced precariously, was Miss Mischief, meowing helplessly.

"Oh for goodness sake!" Abby said.

"She climbed right up the drapes. I know she's fearless, but I don't think she can get down. And I can't reach her."

Abby suspected the kitten would eventually figure a way to return to earth but Mary's distress was far more important than the silly cat's temporary predicament. The survival of the drapes in one piece was also an issue, given the kitten's sharp claws.

"I'll get her." Dragging a kitchen chair into the living room, Abby climbed up to retrieve Miss Mischief. "I think we ought to rename her Miss Trouble."

"I do hope Bobby can find her owner tomorrow," Mary said through clenched teeth.

So did Abby. "I'll put her in the laundry room for now. She'll be safe there and we'll hope for the best tomorrow."

The following morning, Abby pulled on a sweatshirt and her jeans, and went out onto the deck to read her daily devotions. The cool air was invigorating, the sight of the straits beyond the backyard a study in blues and grays.

Reading the devotional about the Israelites coming out of Egypt, she considered that immigrants — both legal and illegal — had a good many reasons to come to America. It was possible Davor Jovanovic, if that was his name, had been persecuted in some other country and was seeking escape and freedom as had so many immigrants to America over the years. Or he could be motivated by some more violent reason. Although most immigrants, she realized, simply came to America to find a better life. It was hard to fault that motivation. Rousing herself from her devotionals, she went inside and ate breakfast with Mary.

"I'm off to Paradise Cove this morning,"

Abby told her sister as they sat at the kitchen table. "It's part of the sparrow inventory I'm doing so we have baseline data to compare to future counts."

Mary gazed at her over the top of her coffee cup. "Are you sure that inventory isn't just an excuse for you to be out tramping through the woods, which has always been your favorite thing to do?"

Abby laughed. "Guilty as charged. I'm the luckiest person in the world to be able to earn a living doing what I love."

Parking her car at the end of the cove, she put on her khaki birding vest so she'd have her binoculars, notebook and digital camera handy. On her clipboard, she had a diagram of the section of the island around the cove where she would conduct her sparrow survey.

As she closed the car door, she heard the distinctive courtship song of a Eurasian skylark. Looking up, she spotted the small bird dipping and looping as he tried to attract the attention of his mate. In a way, this species of skylark was an immigrant, or at least its ancestors were. They'd been introduced on Vancouver Island in Canada in the early 1900s. Since that time, the birds had colonized the San Juan Islands and were now welcome breeding residents.

Smiling, she realized how immigrants of all kinds had added to the rich tapestry of her own experience.

Carrying her clipboard, she walked around the east end of the cove. Along the northern shoreline, boat docks testified to the presence of summer cabins that were nestled in the pine trees and barely visible. Abby couldn't see any sign of life at the moment. Later in the summer this cove would be full of activity.

Beyond the forested area, the landscape changed to low, scrubby brush and grassland, a prime habitat for sparrows. White yarrow blossoms stuck their heads up above the grass while the vines of Oregon manroot competed for space on the ground. Tiny magenta flowers called cranesbill, which looked just like their namesake, hid beside rock outcroppings.

Off to Abby's right, a pair of Savannah sparrows rose out of the grass and fluttered down to the ground quite close to her. That's when Abby realized a young blonde girl of three or four was walking through the grass plucking flowers. She'd flushed the birds from their hiding place.

"Hello there," Abby called.

The child looked up in surprise and froze

as though responding to a 'Simon says stop!' command.

"It's all right." Not wanting to frighten the girl, Abby spoke quietly. "I won't hurt you. What's your name?"

From a nearby stand of trees, a woman's voice called out in a language Abby didn't understand. The only word she caught was Caterina, which she took to be the girl's name.

"I think your mommy is looking for you, Caterina," Abby said, smiling and relieved the child wasn't alone.

The youngster turned and ran toward her mother, a slender woman whose hair was as white-blonde as the child's.

"Hello." Abby called and waved.

Looking as startled as the child had been, the mother hugged her daughter close. Her responding hello sounded tentative, her smile guarded.

"It's a lovely day, isn't it?" Abby persisted.

"Yes. It is nice day," the woman replied, her accent thick. "We must go."

With that, the woman took the child's hand and hurried her back through the trees toward the cabins at the cove.

The brief exchange puzzled Abby. Sparrow Island received a fair number of foreign visitors each year. Usually they were eager to meet and talk with the local residents. The woman she'd just spoken to had seemed almost frightened.

Shrugging, she put her speculation aside and returned to the task of transecting the area she'd decided to survey. By making a *pishing* sound, she enticed a couple of towhee sparrows out from under a clump of shrubs and noted them on her diagram. But after an hour of crisscrossing the open field with minimal sightings, she determined that the sparrow population in the area was not very large. It was possible the closeness of the cabins kept the birds away. Or, more likely, the overall number of seed-eating birds was continuing to decrease on the island.

After finishing the survey, she thought she'd drop in to visit her parents at nearby Stanton Farm. One of the many blessings she'd enjoyed by returning to Sparrow Island was the chance to be near her parents. Both in their eighties, they were in good health and spirits, their faith in God never stronger. Still, Abby liked the idea of being able to check on them frequently.

As she drove down the long driveway to the house, a flock of Savannah sparrows rose up from alongside the road and settled into the adjacent pasture where her father's two dairy cows grazed.

Abby laughed. She'd just traipsed back and forth through a ten-acre parcel of land only to discover the largest population of sparrows literally in her parents' front yard.

Her father had spent years renovating the two-story, wood-and-shingle farmhouse he'd purchased when he and Abby's mother had moved here in 1955. Together they'd made it a home. Abby cherished all of her memories of growing up on the farm, where she'd learned to value both family and all that God had created.

She parked near the back door, walked up the wheelchair ramp that had been installed after Mary's accident and wiped her feet on the stiff straw mat in case there was mud on her shoes.

Knocking first, she pushed open the door. "Anybody home?"

"Come in, dear," her mother called. "I was just making a pot of chicken-vegetable soup to take to Debbie Alder this afternoon. She's not been feeling well and I imagine she doesn't feel like cooking."

Not at all surprised to find Ellen Stanton standing over the stove and planning an act of kindness for a longtime friend, Abby gave her mother a kiss. "Sorry to hear Debbie's ill. Hope it's nothing serious."

"I think she's just getting over a nasty cold. She'll be fine, I'm sure." As always, Ellen's short, curly hair looked as though she'd recently been to the beauty shop, the gray strands neatly in place.

"That's good." Abby sniffed the simmering soup, detecting a hint of thyme. "Smells delicious."

"There's plenty for you to have a bowl, if you're hungry."

Though tempted, Abby declined. "I'd love a cup of tea though."

"Then I'll join you." As Ellen filled the tea kettle, she asked, "Anything in particular bring you here this morning?"

Abby seated herself at the round oak table where she'd eaten so many meals. "Not really. I was nearby at Paradise Cove taking a sparrow inventory and thought I'd drop in, see how you are."

"We're fine, dear. How are the sparrows?"

"I think they've all migrated over here to your cow pasture." Abby chuckled. "I did come across a pretty blonde woman and her young tow-headed daughter while I was doing the survey on the other side of Paradise Cove. The little girl was picking wildflowers. They must be staying in one of the rental cabins. I'm afraid I frightened them off."

"It's early in the season to stay in those cabins. They aren't at all well insulated against our cool nights."

"I imagine that's true. The woman spoke to the little girl in a language I didn't recognize, so they must be foreign visitors. Perhaps when they made the rental arrangements, they weren't familiar with the area."

"That's possible." Ellen got two cups out of the cupboard and set them on the counter. "When someone asks me at the Visitors Center where to stay, I make sure they know what the accommodations are like. There're some rentals that are only suitable for summer use, and the warm part of the summer at that." Twice a week, Ellen volunteered at the center, which was close to the ferry dock where most visitors arrived. She was full of information about where to stay or eat, including camping sites for those who were roughing it.

"What percentage of our visitors would you say are from foreign countries?"

"Oh, let me think. We get a lot of Canadians, of course. They pop over from the mainland or from Vancouver Island. And a growing number of visitors are from Japan and other Asian nations." The teakettle began to steam. Ellen put a tea bag into each of the porcelain cups she'd set on the counter.

Abby thought about the woman she'd spoken to at Paradise Cove as well as the presumably counterfeit documents that claimed Croatian citizenship for their owner.

"How about European visitors?" she asked.

"A fair number of Germans. They appear to be great travelers. Not so many from France, I don't think, and an odd few now and then from England. Why do you ask?"

Briefly, Abby told her about the documents she and Rick had discovered.

"That's troubling."

"If the woman I saw at the cove had been speaking German or French, I wouldn't have necessarily understood her, but I would have recognized the language." Abby had taken French in both high school and college as well as Latin. "The little girl's name is Caterina. What country would that be from?"

Ellen didn't know, and Abby wondered if Caterina was a common name in Croatia.

As Abby was leaving her mother, her cell phone rang. She checked the caller's number. Sergeant Cobb was on the line.

"Hi, Henry. What's up?"

"I reached the Immigration and Customs

agent. He's up to his neck in cases and wonders if you and Rick and I can meet with him in the morning. He works out of the Auburn office, but he has to be at the Border Patrol office in Bellingham tomorrow. He wants to see the documents and hear more about this geocaching business."

"Friday morning? Sure, I think that'd be fine. Do you want me to call Rick?"

"If you don't mind."

"No problem." She agreed they'd meet Henry on the early ferry out of Green Harbor.

As she snapped her phone closed, she felt a flutter of anticipation. By tomorrow they'd know if the documents were forgeries and possibly why they'd been hidden beneath that cache.

CHAPTER FIVE

The next morning the ferry's ear-splitting horn sounded, trumpeting their departure.

Standing at the railing, Abby watched the water churn at the bow of the big ship as it eased out of Green Harbor. Low-flying sea gulls lingered nearby in hope the powerful propellers would stir up a fish for their breakfast. Just outside the harbor, a pair of cormorants flew only feet above the water, their necks outstretched as they headed for their feeding grounds.

Aloud, Abby quoted a Bible verse that came to mind. "And God said, 'Let the water teem with living creatures, and let birds fly above the earth across the expanse of the sky' " (Genesis 1:20).

Next to her, his hands braced on the railing, Henry Cobb said a quiet, "Amen."

Smiling, she glanced up at him. Because the early morning air was cool, he had on his dark green uniform jacket, and his campaign hat was settled squarely on his head. The presence of his weapon on his hip and a briefcase in his hand made him look very official.

"I'm sorry Rick couldn't make it this morning. He's got an engine overhaul to do for a gentleman who's planning to take out his boat this weekend. He said we could call him if the federal agent had any questions we couldn't answer."

"Shouldn't be a problem."

Abby had chosen to wear a tailored pants suit this morning, and the jacket wasn't as warm as she might have liked.

"Can I treat you to a cup of coffee?" she asked.

"Best offer I've had all day. But why don't you be my guest this time? You and Mary are always having me over for dinner."

"That's because we enjoy your company." Her sister was clearly smitten with Henry, which delighted Abby. She liked Henry and he made Mary happy.

Together, they walked into the main cabin. The early ferry was always crowded with commuters en route to their jobs on the mainland. Abby counted herself fortunate her daily commute to the Nature Museum took about fifteen minutes tops.

They joined a line of passengers at the

food service counter, some of whom were buying breakfast. A short-order cook turned out eggs, bacon and pancakes with a quick flick of his wrist, then moved on to the next order. The smells were delicious.

"Did you have breakfast?" Henry asked.

"A bowl of Mary's special granola mix and wheat toast."

"I think I'll get bacon and eggs. I didn't take the time to eat before I left."

As they were standing in line, Neil McDonald came striding across the cabin dressed in his dark blue Washington State Ferry coveralls and orange life vest, regulation gear for ferry workers.

"Good morning, Abby. Henry. Taking a day off in the big city?"

"Business, I'm afraid," Henry said, shaking hands with Abby's neighbor. The two men were about the same height, but Neil was a bit broader across the shoulders, his hands thicker and calloused from hauling the heavy lines the ferry used for docking.

The waiting customers moved forward, and Henry gave the clerk his order.

"You oughta have Yousef make you one of his omelets," Neil suggested. "They're so fluffy, they practically float off the plate."

Henry appeared skeptical, so Neil called to the short-order cook. "Yousef, I'd like you to meet a couple of my good friends."

The cook turned around. When he spotted Henry, his eyes flared briefly and then he smiled, although Abby thought it looked a little forced.

Neil introduced them to Yousef Zeklos. "Yousef and his family moved to Sparrow Island recently. They're from Romania."

"Welcome to America," Abby said.

"Thank you. We are very happy to be here." A slender man in his forties, he had light brown hair that was cut short on top and shaved on the sides. Although his English was good, he spoke with an accent.

"The omelet sounds great," Henry decided, changing his order. "Can you do mushrooms and cheese?"

"Of course." With a curt nod, he turned back to his stove and cracked an egg into a bowl one handed.

Abby accepted a paper cup of coffee from the clerk and stepped back out of the way so Henry could pay.

"By any chance, are Yousef and his family renting a cabin out by Paradise Cove?" she asked Neil.

He rubbed his calloused hand over his chin. "Yeah, maybe. I'm not sure."

"I met, or at least said hello to a woman and her daughter when I was out there yesterday. She dashed off so fast, I was afraid I'd frightened her."

"I know he's got a little girl. Carries her picture in his wallet." He grinned sheepishly. "I was showing off a picture of Bobby and he pulled out a snapshot of his wife and daughter. The girl's name is Caterina. He really dotes on that kid."

"I'm sure he does, and it sounds like the family I met."

"Maybe his wife was uncomfortable because she hasn't been in the country long. I'm not sure how good her English is."

Abby supposed that could be true, but something else was bothering her. She lowered her voice. "Do you think Yousef has a green card?"

Neil looked surprised by her question. "You can bet the ferry system checks out all their employees. They wouldn't hire an undocumented worker, if that's what you're getting at."

Wouldn't *knowingly* hire, Abby mentally added.

She waved off her own comment. "Don't mind me. There've been a lot of stories about illegal immigrants in the news lately. In fact, Henry and I are on our way to talk to an immigration agent about some documents we think may be forged." She told him about geocaching and the find.

"Sandy told me you'd gotten into that hobby," he said of his wife. "She thinks Bobby would enjoy giving it a try. Not that he doesn't already have plenty of hobbies."

She chuckled. Bobby was such a bright boy, his interests were scattered and he thrived on trying new things. "He'd like the treasure hunting. For him, it'd be like searching for pirate's gold!" she teased.

A smile lit Neil's cinnamon-brown eyes. "If he finds any, I hope he shares it with his old man." Neil sobered. "Yousef seems to be a really nice guy. I can't see him as a criminal."

"I didn't intend to accuse him of anything. Really. As you say, the ferry system would be especially cautious about who they hire."

"You got that right." He glanced at his watch. "I gotta get back to work. Maybe I'll catch you on your return trip to Sparrow Island."

Abby told him that would be nice. But even as she sat down at a table and sipped her coffee while Henry ate and raved about his fluffy omelet, she wondered if Yousef Zeklos and his family could have something to hide.

That would explain why the woman she'd met had seemed frightened, and why Yousef had seemed unsettled by seeing Henry in his deputy sheriff's uniform.

Agent Matt Burns had agreed to meet them at the US Border Patrol office located near the Bellingham Golf Course and Country Club. A man in his thirties with closely cropped dark brown hair and a five o'clock shadow, he ushered Abby and Henry into a dingy interview room. He wore a blue windbreaker with the words POLICE and ICE on the back.

"Sorry about the accommodations." He gestured them to the straight-back chairs at a small, scarred table. "The conference room is busy, so we'll have to make do."

"We won't keep you long, Agent Burns." Henry waited until Abby was seated, then sat in the chair next to her, placing his hat on the table. Burns sat across from them.

"So let's see what you've got," he said.

From his briefcase, Henry retrieved the metal tube containing the IDs and slid the documents out.

"We checked for fingerprints but they were clean," Henry said. "DMV doesn't have any record of issuing a license to Davor Jovanovic and the Social Security number belonged to a woman who died two years ago. I had the Seattle police check out the address on the driver's license. It's phony too."

A frown pulled his dark brows together as Burns picked up the green card, examined the front then turned it over. "I'd say it's an exceptional counterfeit job, but let me check to make sure."

He had an electronic device a bit longer and heavier than a TV remote that he held with a pistol grip and swiped the card.

"All the information on the card is supposed to be encrypted on this magnetic strip on the back," he explained. "That's been the hardest part for counterfeiters to duplicate. The problem is, you need special equipment to read the strip and these gadgets are expensive. Only a few government agencies have bought them so far. Generally, employers skip it altogether and just assume the alien registration card is legit."

He slid the green card into the slot. "It's phony, all right. There's nothing there to be read."

"Are there a lot of these forged documents around?" Abby asked.

"Most aren't this good." He placed the green card back on the table. "There're a couple of highly skilled forgery rings operating that could do this good a job, one in

Texas and another in New Jersey. I haven't heard of anybody operating the scam on the West Coast, which doesn't mean the syndicate hasn't expanded.

"Buying these babies isn't cheap, maybe several thousand dollars a pop. Ordinary illegals just looking for work here don't have the bucks to pay a coyote to get 'em across the border and have money left over for this kind of documentation."

"So this Davor fellow is highly motivated and has some financial resources at his disposal," Henry suggested.

"I'd say so." Burns leaned back in his chair, directing his attention to Abby. "Tell me again how you happened to find this stash, Dr. Stanton."

Briefly, she explained geocaching and how she and Rick had found this particular site. Meanwhile, Henry got out the plastic container with the log and fishing lure, and Agent Burns studied the contents.

"We did get a partial print off the fishing lure," Henry said. "But we weren't able to match it to any database. All the prints on the written log were blurred."

"It might help if I showed you the geocaching Web site," Abby suggested. "If you have a computer with Internet access, it would take only a minute or two."

"Good idea."

Burns led them into a large room filled with a half-dozen desks. Only one was occupied at the moment by a mature woman wearing civilian clothes.

"Caroline, can you get us onto the Internet on your computer?" Burns asked. "There's something I'd like Dr. Stanton to show me."

Her head snapped up and she nailed the agent with a peeved look, then shrugged. "Sure. Why not?" With a few quick key strokes, the Internet appeared on her computer screen. Caroline scooted back from the desk and stood.

"Sorry to interrupt your work," Abby said.

"I'm due for a break anyway. If you want, you can write up the reports for these clowns." She aimed a dismissive gesture toward the empty desks in the room. "They wouldn't know the difference."

Slipping into the chair Caroline had just vacated, Abby sent up a quick prayer asking the Lord to help the woman find the sense of peace and contentment that she apparently lacked.

In moments, Abby had the geocaching home page up on the screen. "There are several of these sites," she explained as Agent Burns pulled up a chair beside her.

"Overall, there are some three hundred and fifty thousand geocaches placed in more than two hundred countries around the world. Considering this hobby only started a few years ago when Global Positioning Systems were made available to the general public, it's shown amazing growth.

"At this Web site, I can search for caches by ZIP code to find the ones in the San Juan Islands, which is what we did to find the one we brought you." Again, a few clicks and she showed him the listing.

"This cache was hidden by someone called HeeHaw. When I do a search of his screen name, it shows he's a regular cacher here in the Northwest. But there's no way to tell his real name or any clues that he also planted the container with the fake IDs."

"Would the owner of the site know this guy's real name?" Burns asked.

"Assuming he used a real name when he registered, yes."

"Anything unusual about the way he posted the information, a code you don't recognize?"

Abby shook her head. "It looks entirely legitimate to me. Just like thousands of other postings."

"Then how would Davor Jovanovic know

to look for the IDs he's probably paid big bucks for in that particular cache?"

Abby didn't have an answer for that, nor did Henry.

"Do you think Jovanovic's already living on Sparrow Island?" Henry asked.

"Possibly. Or it might be he hasn't arrived in the country yet."

"I think I need some blow-ups of the guy's photo so I can spread them around to my deputies." Henry had moved around to lean on the partition that separated the secretary's work space from the other desks. "I'd like my deputies to keep an eye out for the man."

"I'd like a copy too," Abby said. "I don't want to stumble across him while I'm doing field work and be caught off guard."

Burns nodded. "I'll get the photo scanned and send you an e-mail."

"If Jovanovic goes looking for his phony IDs and doesn't find them, he's going to be upset," Abby pointed out, handing the agent one of her business cards. "He'll assume his source took his money and didn't fulfill the deal, or that the cache site was muggled."

"Muggled?" Burns echoed, his brows jumping.

"A muggler is someone who isn't involved in geocaching. He or she finds whatever's been hidden and takes it away. Usually a geocacher will post that information on the Web site so the cache owner can replace the cache."

"So Jovanovic might get back to his source via that Web site?" the agent asked.

"I don't know. Maybe."

Agent Burns leaned back in his chair and studied the screen from a distance. "I'm going to have to get a computer analyst to take a look. Problem is, we're shorthanded in that job classification. Computer geeks can make a lot more money in private industry than they can with Homeland Security. It'll take me a while to get someone assigned to the job."

By that time, Abby mused, Davor Jovanovic would be long gone and there could well be more false documents hidden elsewhere.

Abby wished there was a way for her to move the investigation along more rapidly. This was a far more complex scheme than someone standing on a street corner selling cheaply made false IDs. She sensed more was at stake than an undocumented immigrant simply wanting to land a job.

She had to find someone with the time and expertise to search for clues on the Internet.

She also thought it would be smart to get better acquainted with Yousef Zeklos and his family. As recent arrivals in America, they might be able to provide insight. Providing them with an official welcome to Sparrow Island would help break the ice.

By midafternoon on Friday, the pre-weekend spurt of activity at Island Blooms had slowed, which gave Mary a chance to properly file the orders that had been called in that morning.

Candace Grover, the shop manager, appeared from the back workroom carrying two floral arrangements. As usual, she wore a smock over her colorful dress. Her long strawberry-blonde hair hung nearly to her waist.

"I think I'm all caught up," she said. "We've got these two orders that'll be picked up about five o'clock, and that should be it unless someone else calls in." Using her elbow, she slid open the door of the large walk-in refrigerator where flowers were kept fresh. It was chock full of vases filled with roses, tulips, irises, baby's breath, lily of the valley, daisies and other flowers.

"It's been a good day." Mary wheeled back away from the front counter, which caused Finnegan, who'd been lying near her feet, to stand and shake himself, then stretch. "I took several orders for flowers to be sent to the mainland, and we've got three arrangements ordered for tomorrow morning."

"Great." Stepping out of the refrigerator, Candace slid the door closed again. "I've got a half dozen of the dried wreaths for the Best of Sparrow Island Festival ready to go. I thought I'd make up some dried arrangements too."

"That'd be lovely. You have such an artistic knack with dried flowers, your arrangements always sell well."

A pleased flush shot color to Candace's cheeks. "If you need to run any errands, or go on home, I think I can handle the rest of the afternoon by myself."

"I do want to run out to Goldie Landon's place to remind her we'll need a good selection of her orchids for the festival."

Her friend Goldie, a shy, almost reclusive woman in her seventies, lived on the north side of the island. She loved flowers as much as Mary did and had the green thumb to prove it. Not only was her yard beautifully landscaped, she raised exquisite orchids in her own greenhouse on the property.

"You go ahead then," Candace said. "Everything's under control here."

Mary agreed. She was enormously grateful to have such a capable and talented person as her manager. With each passing day, Candace grew more comfortable with the business side of the flower shop and had added her own personality to the displays. From Mary's perspective, it was a perfect arrangement.

She gathered up her purse and some paperwork, told Candace good-bye and headed north in her van. Finnegan sat behind her, watching expectantly out the windshield.

Goldie's house was set well back from the road and overlooked the ocean. To avoid obstructing the view, she'd built the hothouse on the front of her property near the road. A profusion of exotic plants filled the yard and surrounded the greenhouse.

Mary pulled up beside the glass-enclosed structure and got out of the van. With Finnegan's assistance, she followed a path to the entrance. Despite the door standing wide open, the inside temperature was about eighty degrees, the humidity above forty percent. Instantly a fine sheen of perspiration formed above Mary's lip. The light sweater she wore suddenly felt too warm.

She spotted her friend working at the far end of the building.

"Goodness, I must remember to come visit you next winter when we have a cold snap." She wheeled between a row of tables laden with orchids. Some of the blooms were delicate shades of blue and lavender, others were white on spidery vines and dozens displayed the more familiar purple flower. Together, they scented the air with a tropical perfume.

"Mary! It's good to see you." The petite woman welcomed her with a warm smile. Her white hair looked slightly disheveled and she appeared somewhat fragile, but her eyes sparkled with pleasure.

Despite the muddy gloves Goldie wore, Mary held out her arms and they exchanged hugs.

"How are you, Goldie?"

"I'm quite well, thank you. Keeping myself busy."

"Looks to me like you've been doing far more than just keeping busy. Your plants are gorgeous."

Looking around with pride, Goldie nodded. "There's an orchid show in Seattle in a few weeks. I think I'm just about ready."

"I'll say." Carefully, Mary fingered a delicate purple petal. "You haven't forgotten our local festival, I hope?"

"Not at all. I've been repotting some of the plants today and they'll be more than ready by Father's Day weekend." She walked back down the aisle and Mary followed. "I enjoy doing the local festival. People are always so surprised we can raise orchids right here on Sparrow Island."

"It amazes me too. Just coming in here is like being transported to the South Pacific."

"Without all the hassle of crowded airports and rude taxi drivers." Chuckling softly, Goldie poked at the dirt around a plant she'd just repotted. "Not that I've traveled all that much, of course."

Mary imagined Goldie was far more comfortable with herself for company than with meeting strangers. Her orchids certainly thrived as a result of Goldie's undivided attention.

They talked a while about how many orchids and which varieties Goldie should provide for the festival. Of course, if they sold out of any particular variety on the first day, she'd be able to restock overnight.

By the time Mary left, it was time to get home and give some thought to fixing supper.

She also wanted to find out if Bobby had discovered the owner of little Miss Mischief.

She'd had to leave the kitten in the laundry room when she left the house. Mary doubted Miss Mischief had been happy about that. But surely Blossom was relieved, and the drapes and knickknacks around the house had been safe from the kitten's rambunctious behavior.

That little kitty certainly needed a suitable home of her own.

CHAPTER SIX

Abby returned to Sparrow Island by ferry, still troubled by the counterfeit documents and why Davor Jovanovic — if that was his real name — was so anxious to buy expensive immigration papers. Had he tried to come to the country legally and been turned away? If so, why? And what was he planning to do in America?

Henry dropped her off at her car, which she'd parked at the ferry terminal. She wanted to stop at the Nature Museum to get her messages before she went home.

She arrived to find the parking lot nearly empty and Wilma Washburn, the conservatory's receptionist, secretary and general go-to gal, starting to lock up the two-story building for the day.

"Hi, Wilma." Abby scooted in through the large glass-and-chrome door as Wilma held it open for her. "Busy day?"

"The further we get into June, the more

tourists we get. If today was an example of what summer's going to be like, we'll set a record for this year." The gray-haired woman twisted the key in the lock and tested the door. "I've already had to reorder some of the San Juan birding books for our gift shop."

"That's good. Sounds like I may have a lot of takers for my weekly bird walks."

"A whole bunch signed up for tomorrow. You may need an assistant at the back of the line to keep them moving."

"Fortunately, I scheduled a couple of our volunteers who are pretty knowledgeable birders to help." She walked over to the reception counter and picked up the clipboard with the sign-up sheet for the eight o'clock walk. In front of the counter were piles of Wilma's intricate handwoven baskets, a skill that had been handed down from her Native American ancestors. The baskets were popular items in the museum's gift shop and at Bayside Souvenirs, where Wilma had them on consignment.

"You must have worked the entire winter to make so many baskets," Abby commented.

Always jovial, Wilma laughed. "They're not all mine. Some of the other ladies in my tribe have been making baskets for the Best of Sparrow Island Festival. They brought them by today, and my nephew's going to pick them up tomorrow and take them to the Dorset to store them."

Picking up a small basket from the pile, Abby studied the complicated design of overlapping diamonds. "Amazing. I don't know how you have the patience to weave dried grass and strips of cedar into such detailed patterns."

"Practice, practice, practice." Selecting a medium-sized basket from the second stack, Wilma turned it over and showed Abby the underside. "This one was made by a woman I don't know. That's her mark there."

Abby nodded.

"The problem is, this basket isn't very well made. The weave isn't tight and it's not really a traditional pattern." She bent the side of the basket to show the loose weave.

"Maybe the woman's new to weaving."

"Possibly." Tossing the basket back on the stack, Wilma shifted her long hair behind her shoulder. Her name tag was pinned on the pocket of her khaki blouse. "Some native tribes, like the Navajos in the Four Corners area of Arizona and Utah, have had trouble with people selling crafts, claiming they're Native American made when, in fact, they're knock-offs manufactured in

China or some other country that has cheap labor."

"You think the one you showed me is fake?"

"I don't know. Imported baskets are supposed to have a tag on the back indicating where they were made. But it's easy to pull the tag off and put your own mark on it."

"You're right. I've seen those flimsy stickers."

"Our baskets are far more expensive than the imported ones, and for good reason. If someone spent a lot of money for a fake and found out, they'd be terribly upset."

"Rightfully so." Abby picked up the basket in question, thinking the world was suddenly filled with counterfeiters. "How many of these did the woman bring in?"

"Only three. But she didn't bring them in, she sent them by UPS from San Juan Island. I tried to call her, but her phone isn't listed. All I have is her address."

"Lots of people have unlisted phone numbers. It's even possible she doesn't have a phone. But I see your dilemma."

Wilma went behind the counter and pulled her purse out of a drawer. "I think I'll ask around first. If I can't find anyone who can vouch for her, I may have to go over to San Juan Island myself and check on her. I feel it's my responsibility to make sure when I claim something's made by a Native American, that it is." She slung the purse strap over her shoulder. "If you don't need anything from me, I'll be on my way home."

"I'm fine. Just dropped by to pick up my messages."

Wilma wished her a good evening, then headed toward the back of the building to let herself out.

Abby walked through the door marked PRIVATE that separated the public areas of the museum from the offices and workroom. She saw her boss Hugo Baron still at his desk and stopped to say hello.

"You're working late this evening," she said.

He glanced up and smiled. As always, the conservatory curator was dressed impeccably in a hand-tailored suit and matching silk tie. His snow-white hair and mustache were well groomed, adding the perfect note of sophistication.

"Just catching up on some correspondence with an old friend in Kenya," he said. Evidence of his world travels lined his office. Among Abby's favorites were a photo of him with a group of Masai tribesmen and a drawing of a moose on birch bark created by an Alaskan native. "How did your visit go with the immigration people?"

Once again, Abby was grateful for how flexible Hugo was regarding her schedule at the conservatory. He'd quickly agreed when she had told him about the meeting in Bellingham.

"The ICE agent wasn't as helpful as I might have hoped, but he did say the documents we found were counterfeit."

"*Hmm,* you suspected as much."

"Suspicion confirmed, I'm afraid." She walked into his office and sat in the leather chair in front of his desk. The day had been long and stressful. Her mind raced with questions. "What do you know about Romania?"

Hugo's deep blue eyes widened in surprise. "I thought the documents indicated Croatia was the gentleman's place of birth."

"The forged documents, yes. But I met a man on the ferry who recently arrived from Romania." She told him about Yousef and that his family lived near Paradise Cove.

Listening thoughtfully, Hugo tented his fingers under his chin.

When she finished, he said, "Interesting. As for my knowledge of Romania, it's a very ancient culture that dates back some two million years. The early settlers created some remarkable polychrome pottery."

"I was actually thinking of more recent history."

"Ah, yes." Recognizing he sometimes got carried away, he chuckled. "Let me see . . . recent history. In the past twenty years, the Romanian economy has grown considerably, democracy is now well rooted, and the country has been admitted to both NATO and the European Union."

Leaning forward, he rested his arms on his desk, which was clear of any clutter except the letter he'd been writing and his pen. "As it happens, the son of a dear friend of mine has a fairly high-level position at the US Embassy in Bucharest. If you should have any specific questions, I'm sure he'd be happy to answer them."

Abby wasn't surprised Hugo was personally acquainted with high-level diplomats. His travels had taken him around the globe many times, and she doubted he'd ever met a person who remained a stranger for long.

"I am curious why a family would leave Romania and immigrate to America, particularly since you say the Romanian economy is strong. Yousef didn't mention having family in the States." Although it was true Yousef hadn't done much talking at all.

"As a rule, people come to America for

the opportunities the country has to offer. In fact, your new friend is fortunate to have permanent status and is able to work here. The quota for immigrants from Romania must be quite small. Priority is given to those who are reuniting with close relatives already living here. For others, the wait would be long. Unless, of course, he has some special skill that's in short supply in our country and an employer is having difficulty filling a vacancy."

Abby doubted short-order cooks fell into that category, which made her wonder if Yousef had connections to come here legally, or if he'd found another way to move his family to America.

"I think I'll drop by their cabin tomorrow and bring them a welcoming gift. Perhaps something for the little girl would break the ice. It must be hard to be a stranger in a new country." She'd also be able to satisfy her curiosity about Yousef.

"I'm sure they would appreciate the gesture," Hugo said.

Letting Hugo get back to his correspondence, Abby left to check her phone messages and glance through the mail that had been left in her in-box. With nothing pressing at the moment, she decided to head home.

Fifteen minutes later, she arrived at her sister's house to find Mary sitting at the entrance to the laundry room with a dismayed expression on her face.

"What's wrong?"

"Will you just look at what that little rascal did today while she was locked inside." Mary threw up her hands. "I don't know whether to laugh or cry."

Neither did Abby. A roll of paper towels was strung around the room like a banner, a box of detergent had tipped over, spilling the contents, and the laundry basket had been emptied of the clean clothes Abby hadn't yet put away. The clothes themselves looked as though they'd been wadded into a pillow, the mashed spot in the middle a perfect nesting place for a napping kitten.

The kitten was nowhere in sight.

"Where's Miss Mischief now?" Abby asked, unable to keep the laughter from her voice.

"I had Bobby take her and Finnegan outside to play."

"I gather Bobby hasn't discovered where Miss Mischief belongs."

Mary wheeled away from the laundry room door. "I'm afraid not. He said he went to every house up and down our street, and no one owned up to even having seen her, much less claimed her. I'm afraid she truly is a homeless stray."

"It does seem so." Picking up a blouse that the kitten had dragged across the room, Abby tossed it into the laundry basket.

"Abby, I know she's a sweet little thing, and certainly full of vim and vigor, but I just don't think we can keep her. She needs a home with children who can play with her, not two old women who are stuck in their ways."

"Ha! Speak for yourself," Abby teased. "But you're right about us not being suitable owners for such an active kitten. If nothing else, we're not home enough to give her the attention she deserves."

"I suppose we can take her to Dr. Federer. Hopefully, he'll be able to find a good home for her."

The only veterinarian on the island, Dr. Federer was well loved and respected.

"Yes, we may have to do that." Thoughtfully, Abby scooped up the rest of the laundry that would now have to be washed again. "But I have another idea. There's a little girl who's living out by Paradise Cove who could use a playmate. I'd planned to visit them tomorrow anyway. I'll just take Miss Mischief along for the ride. I imagine the little girl will enjoy playing with the kitty."

"It would be even better if they were willing to adopt the little rascal."

"True enough," Abby agreed. "If the family seems at all interested, I'll test the waters."

Mary started to wheel away from the laundry room, then stopped. "I called Keith Gordon about your geocaching event. He says he's always happy to find room for your activities, particularly when it will bring more visitors to the island."

"Oh, good. I'll let Rick know, then I'll post the information on the geocaching Web site. They send out weekly messages to members who live in the area."

The following morning, Abby found more than twenty people gathered beneath the bigleaf maple in front of the Nature Museum waiting for the morning bird walk to begin. Ranging in age from five to eighty-five, most wore light jackets against the cool morning air and many had binoculars dangling around their necks.

Abby wore her khaki birding vest over a long-sleeved shirt and khaki pants with her hiking boots. Not that she planned a very rigorous hike this morning. They'd be keeping to well-groomed conservatory trails.

She stepped up onto the low wall that circled the maple tree, enclosing a bed of blue flowering lithodora. At five foot three, she needed to stand on something in order to be seen by the crowd.

"Good morning, everyone. Welcome to Sparrow Island Nature Conservatory. I'm Abby Stanton, the Associate Curator and resident ornithologist here at the conservatory. But most people simply call me the Bird Lady."

That got a titter of laughter from the crowd.

"I'm being assisted this morning by two of our conservatory volunteers. Feel free to ask them any questions you like as we go along." She indicated the pair, who were standing at the back of the crowd, both proudly wearing their volunteer name tags. They waved to acknowledge her introduction.

"How many of you are experienced birders?" she asked the group.

A few people raised their hands, mostly older couples.

"How many of you would like to learn more about birds and how to identify them?"

Virtually everyone raised their hand,

except a teenage boy who was engrossed in some electronic device he was holding. A typical teen dragged here by his parents, she suspected. She mentally vowed that by the end of the walk she'd get him interested.

She gave the birders a brief history of the conservatory and told them they'd be seeing only a portion of the grounds on this morning's walk, and invited them to return to investigate other areas on their own.

"We'll start off walking through a relatively dry forest area of lodgepole pines, fir and more of these beautiful bigleaf maples." She gestured to the tree they were standing under. "With any luck we'll see wrens, red crossbills and Cooper's hawks, and perhaps some less frequent visitors to the conservatory grounds. Then we'll make our way to the shoreline where my favorite heron and a lot of shorebirds hang out. If you'll follow me . . ."

With that, she made her way through the crowd and picked up her pace toward the path into the conservatory grounds. She had learned long ago when leading a crowd to keep moving briskly or people would dawdle. The volunteer docents would try to keep those at the back from losing touch with the rest of the group.

There were several predetermined spots

where she always stopped. One had a great view of a bald eagle nest. Another was a good site where house wrens invariably scolded those who encroached on their territory, and visitors loved it.

Of course, she had to keep an eye out for the unexpected, and often spotted sparrows darting in and out of the undergrowth or a raven soaring overhead.

By the time the group reached the shoreline and were enjoying the marine birds, she noticed that the teenager with his handheld gadget had moved away from the others. Her curiosity piqued, she strolled over to him.

"Whatever you've got there must be fascinating," she commented.

His face flushed, and she could see early signs of adolescent whiskers burgeoning on his chin. "Yeah. It's okay."

"What is it?"

"It's, ah, you know, a GPS."

"Really? Are you by any chance a geocacher?"

He grinned and seemed to relax. "You know about that stuff?"

"I do. I've got a friend who owns one of those. We've managed to find a few caches here on the island."

"There's supposed to be one around here

someplace, but I haven't spotted it yet. I maybe got the coordinates wrong."

That was interesting. Usually a cacher would get permission from a property owner before hiding the cache. As far as she knew, no one had requested the conservatory's permission, and that was troubling.

She asked the young man which Web site he used. It happened to be the same one she checked regularly, but before she had time to delve deeper, a couple from California came over to ask her questions about the sandpipers that were foraging along the low tide line.

After that, it was time to officially end the morning's walk. She invited them to stay to enjoy the scenery or return to the museum to view the exhibits.

When she started to head back, she realized the teenager had already left, and she didn't know if he had found the cache or not. She would have to check the Web site and try to find it herself. But now she wanted to welcome the Romanian family to the island.

Returning to her office, Abby retrieved Miss Mischief from an oversized wire cage she used when rehabilitating birds. She'd placed the kitten there for safe keeping, along with toys and a couple of soft towels to make a nest for napping.

Picking up the kitten and giving her a good pet, Abby slipped her into a portable cat carrier and secured the latch.

There were a half-dozen cabins on the north side of Paradise Cove. Abby wasn't entirely certain which cabin the Zeklos family was renting. She drove slowly along the road, glancing at each cabin for signs of activity. Finally she spotted a little pink scooter and knew she'd found the right place. She pulled over to park behind a small Ford compact.

She'd put together a basket of fruit, some of Mary's homemade cookies, a tin of herbal tea she especially enjoyed and topped everything off with a coloring book and crayons for the little girl. Of course, she hoped Miss Mischief would be the real ice-breaker.

As she picked up the cat carrier, the kitten issued a disgruntled meow.

"Hush, little lady. I want you to make a good impression on the Zeklos family."

A narrow path led to the cabin. Smoke drifted up from a chimney on a steep roof that was shaded by lodgepole pines and a large fir tree. A small, covered porch was flanked by a window on each side. Setting the cat carrier down, Abby knocked on the front door.

After a few moments, the door opened. Yousef Zeklos, dressed in jeans and a flannel shirt, gave her a wary look. "Yes?"

"Hello. I'm Abby Stanton. Neil Mc-Donald introduced us yesterday on the ferry. I thought I'd drop by to officially welcome you and your family to Sparrow Island."

His gaze slid past her as though expecting someone to be lurking behind her.

"You wish to welcome us?" The concept seemed foreign to him.

"Yes, I saw your wife and daughter out walking the other day, but we didn't have a chance to talk." She held up the basket. "I brought a little gift."

His attention dropped to the basket and the hint of a smile lifted the corners of his lips. "Crayons for my Caterina. Please, you come in, yes?"

He opened the door wider and called to his wife in their native language.

Picking up the cat carrier with her free hand, Abby stepped inside as the slender blonde she recognized from their prior encounter appeared from the kitchen. Young Caterina clung to her mother's skirt.

"This is my wife Ileana and my daughter

Caterina." He beckoned his family closer. "Ms. Abby Stanton has brought us a present."

"Please, call me Abby. It's very nice to meet you both."

Ileana smiled shyly. "It is nice to meet you too."

Abby handed her the basket. "There's something in there for Caterina."

"My daughter is just learning English," Yousef said.

Squatting so she was at eye level with the little girl, Abby asked, "How old are you?" She held up four fingers.

Caterina nodded and mimicked Abby's gesture. "Four years old," she whispered.

Just then Miss Mischief decided she was missing out on all the fun and let her presence be known by clawing wildly at the carrier.

Caterina's baby blue eyes brightened, her little face glowed with excitement and she pointed at the kitty, talking hurriedly to her parents.

Standing, Abby explained that the cat was a stray and she thought their daughter would enjoy playing with the kitten for a little while.

While Abby was explaining the situation, Caterina ventured close to the carrier and slipped her fingers inside to pet Miss Mischief. It was clearly love at first sight. Mischief rewarded her new friend with a purr loud enough to be heard across the room.

Ileana made eye contact with her husband, who gave a small nod of approval.

"You say this cat is a stray?" Yousef asked.

"I'm afraid so," Abby said.

"Would you be looking to find a new home for this cat?"

Abby smiled with relief. "I'd love to find her a good home, but I don't want you to feel you have to take her."

"I think, yes, our Caterina would say we must do this." Looking pleased, he nodded his approval.

"Please, you sit down," Ileana said. "I fix some tea for you."

The furniture came with the rental and showed heavy wear from years of use by vacationers. The ribbing around the cushions on the couch was frayed, the end table had a dozen nicks and scratches and an equal number of water-stained rings. It was also obvious that Ileana worked hard to keep the cabin neat and clean for her family.

The one addition to the vacation decor seemed to be an exquisite bronze crucifix that was mounted on the wall. A family heirloom, Abby guessed. Another was a chipped dinner plate filled with what appeared to be Easter eggs decorated in the traditional Romanian fashion with bright colors, striking geometric designs and stylized flowers. *Surely the eggs aren't real, not this many months after Easter.*

With her father's permission, Caterina released Miss Mischief from her cage and held her gently. The kitten nudged her chin, which drew a high-pitched giggle from the little girl.

"I put a box of cat food in the carrier," Abby said. "Just to get you started, if you decide to keep the kitty."

"I think my daughter has already decided this question for us." Yousef's indulgent smile confirmed that Caterina was the apple of her father's eye and that Miss Mischief had found a new home.

Ileana returned from the kitchen with a tray of steaming cups and a plate of Mary's cookies. She set the tray on the table next to the couch where Abby was sitting.

"Does the cat have a name?" she asked.

Abby was sure Miss Mischief would get into far less trouble with the Zekloses than she had at Mary's house and her name would no longer be appropriate.

"Why don't you let Caterina name her?" Abby suggested. "That way the kitty will know she belongs here."

"Yes, that would be good." Ileana smiled at her daughter.

While Caterina played with the kitten, the grownups sipped their tea and tried to make small talk.

"These cookies are very good," Ileana said. "Much butter."

"Yes, my sister is a wonderful cook."

"In this family, it is Yousef who is the good cook." Ileana sent her husband a fond look.

He gave a quick shake of his head. "No longer."

Abby wondered why he'd deny he was a good cook, but sensed he didn't want to discuss the subject. "Are you folks from Bucharest? I understand it's a lovely city. I've always wanted to visit."

"Bucharest is very nice, yes," Ileana said. "But America is much nicer."

Curious, Abby pointed at the attractive display of eggs. "Did you paint those eggs?" she asked Ileana.

The blonde nodded and color rose to her cheeks. "They are not real eggs. They are rocks Caterina and I collect on the beach. And then . . ." She shrugged. "I paint them because they remind me of home. My

110

grandmother taught me how and someday I will teach Caterina."

"They're beautiful. May I?" Abby reached for an egg, or rather a water-rounded rock painted with a careful red zigzag design overlayed by a stylized yellow daisy. The artistry was quite extraordinary she thought as she weighed the stone in her palm. "You're very talented, Ileana."

"My grandmother was much more skilled. This I do just to pass the time." She glanced up at her husband, and again they communicated something that Abby couldn't ascertain.

Although Abby asked a few more questions about their past and how they had decided to come to America, both Yousef and his wife seemed reluctant to talk about themselves.

"I know Caterina isn't old enough to go to school," Abby said, thinking of another way to make the family feel at home in their new country. "But she might enjoy attending the Sunday school at my church." She told them about Little Flock and where it was located on the other side of Green Harbor. "And if she likes the Sunday school, we have a Vacation Bible School starting Monday that she could attend. I'm sure she'd have fun with the other children and it would probably help her learn English."

"We are members of the Romanian Orthodox Church," Yousef said cautiously.

"Everyone's welcome at Little Flock. It's entirely up to you."

Yousef and his wife communicated an unspoken message with their eyes, then he said, "It is possible we will visit your church. We will see what is best for us."

CHAPTER SEVEN

When it was time to leave the Zekloses, Abby got in her car and waved good-bye to the family as they stood on their front porch, the kitty held firmly and lovingly in Caterina's arms.

With the problem of the energetic kitten happily resolved, Abby turned her attention back to the false documents she and Rick had found.

How on earth was she going to find time to search through several Web sites and potentially thousands of postings to find references to Davor Jovanovic or a trail that led to him? There had to be some way to narrow the search. But what?

The one person she knew in Green Harbor who was a whiz with computers was Aaron Holloway.

She smiled to herself, and turned her car toward town.

A young man in his mid-twenties and a

relative newcomer to the island, Aaron worked for his grandfather at Holloway's Hardware. Though initially he didn't know much about the hardware business, he knew enough about computers to set up a system to track inventory, pay bills and send out invoices. His grandfather had been thrilled. And as time passed, Aaron had begun taking on more responsibility for running the store, leaving Frank Holloway more time to share fishing tales with his cronies, who loitered on the store's front porch on warm summer mornings.

Abby found a parking place just a couple of stores away from Holloway's.

At the moment, the rustic chairs and old bench on the porch were empty, so she went inside. To her surprise, she found Mary near the cash register talking with Aaron.

"Fancy meeting you here," she said.

Mary wheeled around, her expression as surprised as Abby was. "Well, hi, yourself. I didn't know you were coming to Holloway's today." At her side, Finnegan wagged his greeting too.

"I didn't know either until a few minutes ago. Hi, Aaron. Looks like you're a popular young man today."

A blush crept up his neck to his cheeks, and he brushed his long hair back from his face. "Mary was just asking me about guys who do fancy woodworking and might like to sell their stuff at the Best of Sparrow Island Festival."

"Oh, good idea, Mary. Did you come up with any names, Aaron?"

"Yeah, a couple. Ed Thornly's been making kids' rocking chairs the old-fashioned way. You know, he uses wooden dowels and glue instead of nails 'n stuff and then stains 'em. Real classy. There's another guy, Art Bentley, who makes jigsaw puzzles that are pretty cool. I figured I could ask them if they're interested."

"They both sound like good additions to the festival to me," Abby said.

"I agree," Mary said. "So my business with Aaron is done for now and he's all yours. I hope you're not here because something's broken at home and we have to fix it."

"Oh no, nothing like that. I'm hoping to enlist Aaron's help for some Internet research."

Aaron brightened, the thought of research apparently appealing. "What do you need?"

A customer carrying a can of paint approached them. Abby stepped aside so he could get to the counter to make his purchase. Holloway's carried almost everything imaginable for home repairs and maintenance, from tools and paint to hot water heaters. Rarely did a local homeowner have to travel to the mainland to get what he needed.

While Aaron was ringing up the sale on the cash register, Mary asked, "How'd it go with the new family?"

"They loved your cookies *and* Miss Mischief. The little girl took to the kitten right off, and her parents approved."

"Oh, thank goodness! Blossom can come out from her hiding place now. I do believe her nose was quite put out of joint by having another cat in the house."

Abby chuckled. "Well, she can relax now. And Mischief is in very good hands."

Deciding she should be on her way, Mary told Abby that she'd see her later at home and waved good-bye to Aaron, who was finishing up with his customer.

Abby waited until the gentleman stepped away from the counter before explaining the situation to Aaron and telling him what kind of help she needed.

"Wow! I read a newspaper article about geocaching not too long ago, and it sounded interesting. But who knew the whole geocaching business would be subverted by some big counterfeiting ring? They oughta

116

be stopped."

"I'm going to try to reach the owner of the Web site," Abby said. "I'm hoping he'll reveal the contact information for someone who's using the screen name of HeeHaw, the person who originally planted the cache. But the owner may demand a court order before he shares anything personal about a registered member who uses his site."

"If there're e-mail addresses available, I may be able to track them back to their Internet providers."

"That would be great. I'm also wondering if there's a way to search the Web site for patterns, like other caches HeeHaw has planted. Or maybe unusual comments that cachers have made that could indicate there's something more at a specific location than meets the eye."

Thoughtfully, Aaron brushed his straight hair away from his face again. "That may take some work, but I'll see what I can do."

"I can't ask any more than that of you."

"I won't be able to work on it here at the store. Too many interruptions. But I'll have some free time tonight and tomorrow."

"Hope I'm not ruining your plans for the weekend."

"Don't I wish." He grinned sheepishly, a

tacit admission he didn't have a date scheduled.

Abby thought the young women of Sparrow Island were missing a good thing. Aaron was smart and good-looking, with a pretty good future if he took over his grandfather's hardware store someday, which seemed to be Frank Holloway's hope. But she'd noted Aaron was shy around girls, sometimes painfully so. Maybe he was simply a diamond in the rough and as he matured he'd be more comfortable in social settings.

She gave him the information about the Web site and how to register as a member. "Do what you can and get back to me right away if something pops out at you."

"Will do."

A middle-aged man holding a corroded faucet in his hand approached the counter. "You got anything like this?" he asked, holding up the worn plumbing fixture.

"Yes, sir," Aaron responded. "I'd be happy to show you." To Abby he said, "I'll give you a call with what I find out in a day or two."

"Thanks." She watched him walk the customer down the aisle toward plumbing supplies, confidence in his stride. Aaron knew as much as anyone — outside of a computer expert from the industry — about how to maneuver through the tangled roadways of the Internet. If there was anything to learn about the counterfeited documents, given enough time, Aaron would find it.

Meanwhile, Abby intended to do a little digging herself.

She drove home and found Mary hadn't returned yet. Blossom had reverted to one of her favorite napping spots and was curled up on an armchair in the living room.

When Abby knelt next to her, Blossom blinked open her electric blue eyes and gazed at her as though expecting an apology for the antics of the recent interloper.

Abby ran her fingers through the cat's long white fur. "You know, you could have been a little more welcoming to Miss Mischief instead of hiding out all the time. She might have learned good manners from you."

Unimpressed with the lecture, Blossom's eyes closed and her chest heaved with a sigh that could only be relief. All was well and the queen of the castle was content to be the sole feline in the household again.

Chuckling to herself, Abby went up to her room.

Sitting down at her desk, she booted up her laptop. With a few quick keystrokes, she reached the geocaching Web site and began to search for all the caches in the San Juan Islands. She read each one, looking for clues, any hint that something beyond a log-book and an inexpensive trinket would be found.

She did find the listing for the cache that had been planted on conservatory grounds. The owner, once again, was HeeHaw, an individual very active in the geocaching world. But who was he?

She e-mailed the owner of the Web site. She told him she needed some information related to a police matter and asked him to call her. She left her cell phone number. Better to talk to him on the phone rather than try to explain the situation in an e-mail. She hoped she'd also get a sense of what kind of a person the owner was and whether he might be involved in the coun-terfeiting ring.

By the time she heard the garage door open for Mary, she'd gotten exactly nowhere in terms of discovering a lead on the fake IDs.

Leaning back in her chair, she took off her glasses and rubbed her eyes. She cer-tainly hoped Aaron would have more luck than she'd had.

■ ■ ■ ■

Sunday morning dawned clear and cool.

Abby bundled up in a warm jacket and went out onto the back deck for her morning devotionals. In the stillness of early morning, with the sound of birds singing and waves humming against the shore, she felt close to God.

Saying a silent prayer that her heart be open to the Lord's message, she opened her book of daily devotions. The biblical quote was from Hebrews 6:19. "We have this hope as an anchor for the soul, firm and secure."

The day's reading was about a family who had struggled both with their health and their finances. But the one thing they had plenty of was hope and dreams for a better future. Eventually those dreams came true.

Holding the book open in her lap, Abby wondered what hopes and dreams had brought the Zeklos family to America. Probably dreams not much different than those her own ancestors had held as much as two hundred years ago when they immigrated to this country.

Closing her eyes, Abby prayed the Zekloses would be as well blessed as the Stanton family and that their future would be as rewarding.

After breakfast, Mary drove them to Little Flock for morning worship services. She wore a full skirt and blouse with a light jacket; Abby had chosen a comfortable pants suit with a paisley blouse with navy and gold swirls.

The weathered metal cross at the peak of the shingled steeple glistened its welcome as Mary turned onto the church's long drive to the parking lot. A mass of red, pink and lavender rhododendrons spilled their blooms over the white picket fence that divided the drive from a spacious lawn at the front of the church. A few children dressed in their Sunday best were playing tag on the grass while grownups visited outside the church entrance before the service commenced.

Parking the van, Mary exited by the lift along with Finnegan, and Abby helped to push the wheelchair toward the open doors of the sanctuary. Their progress was fairly slow as they greeted friends, many of whom they'd known since they were young girls growing up on the island. Abby counted the chance to rejoin her home church as one of the many blessings she'd enjoyed since her return to Sparrow Island.

She glanced around, hoping to see the

Zekloses. When she didn't, she felt a pang of disappointment. Perhaps she'd have a chance to extend the invitation a second time if their paths crossed again.

Inside, Mary wheeled to the pew that Rick DeBow had shortened soon after the accident to accommodate her wheelchair. Ellen and George Stanton were already seated in the pew. The dark wood, smoothed by time, gleamed in the soft light filtered by the stained glass window at the back of the church.

Greeting her parents, Abby sat next to her mother. Finnegan, long used to the routine, lay down on the floor in front of Mary without waiting for the command.

The pianist began playing the prelude. Abby folded her hands in her lap, centering herself and welcoming the comfort of the familiar setting and the Lord's presence settling over her.

The pastor, Rev. James Hale, was a tall, slender man in his early forties with sandy-blond hair, a quick smile and a warm personality. The congregation had come to both love and respect him in the years he, his wife and their two-year-old son had been a part of their lives. His quick wit and sense of humor made his sermons a pleasure to listen to and there was always a lesson to be learned. Today's lesson was about finding your way out of trouble by letting the Lord guide you.

The service ended with one of Abby's favorite hymns, "Lead Me Gently Home, Father." While she didn't have a particularly good singing voice, the music always inspired her.

As they were filing out of the church, Bobby came running over to Mary.

"Hey, Mary! Dad's gonna take me fishing this afternoon. We're gonna try to catch that four pounder the lady from the Tackle Shop told you about."

Mary hooked her arm around Bobby's waist and pulled him close for a one-arm hug. "Goodness. How exciting. A fish that big will be enough to feed the whole neighborhood."

"Oh, we won't kill him. We keep what we catch alive in a special tub of water and take 'em to the marina where the judges can weigh 'em." He broke free from the hug to ruffle Finnegan's coat and scratch him on top of his head. "They're the ones keeping track of all the entries in the Bass Fishing Classic. After they do the weighing, they let the fish go so somebody else can catch him."

"I imagine the fish is happy about being released."

"Yeah, I guess. I gotta go now. Mom says I gotta change clothes before we go fishing. She's gonna pack us a lunch." In an imitation of a miniature whirlwind, Bobby spun around and raced off to join his parents, who were walking toward their car.

Mary laughed. "Bobby's a perfect example of why you should raise your family while you're young. Mercy, but I wouldn't be able to keep up with that boy even if I could walk."

"Maybe the secret is that having children keeps you young whatever your age."

To Abby's delight, she spotted Yousef Zeklos and his wife Ileana, with Caterina walking between them holding their hands. They must have been sitting where Abby's view was blocked.

"Speaking of young families, I want you to meet the family from Romania I told you about." Hurriedly, she pushed Mary along the walkway until she caught up with the trio. "Good morning, Yousef. Ileana."

They halted at the sound of their names being called and turned, their facial expressions composed. When Yousef recognized Abby, he smiled.

"I'm so glad you could come to church this morning," Abby said, shaking his hand

and Ileana's. "I hope you enjoyed the service."

"The service was good, yes," he said. "Not the same as home, but good, I think."

"I'd like you to meet my sister, the cookie baker in our family." Abby made the introductions, and Mary extended her welcome to the family.

"Did Caterina like the Sunday school?"

"Yes, I think so." Because his English was good, Yousef seemed to speak for his family. "We talked to the teacher about your Vacation Bible School. We think Caterina would like that too. We did not know if we could afford the cost. The teacher said there were . . ." He paused, searching for the word he wanted.

"Scholarships?" Mary suggested.

"Yes, that is right. The teacher thought Caterina could attend with a scholarship."

"I'm so glad. She'll have a wonderful time, I'm sure." Abby shifted her attention to the child. "How's your kitty today?"

Barely peeking out from behind her mother's skirt, the child smiled shyly.

"Have you given the kitty a name yet?" Abby asked.

The child whispered a word Abby didn't understand.

"She has named the kitty *Comoară*," Ileana said, helping her daughter out. "It means precious in Romanian. We will probably call her *Como,* for short."

"That sounds like a perfect name," Mary said to Caterina. "Our cat's name is Blossom. Maybe you can come and visit her someday."

At the moment, Caterina seemed far more interested in Finnegan than in the prospect of meeting Blossom.

"Would you like to pet my dog?" Mary asked gently.

Checking first with her father, who nodded his approval, Caterina tentatively placed her hand on top of Finnegan's head. His wagging tail brought a giggle to the little girl's lips and she spoke rapidly to her mother in Romanian.

"She loves animals," Ileana said. "We had a dog in Bucharest. We had to leave him with friends when we came to America." Ileana pressed her lips together as though trying not to let the memory hurt too much.

Abby ached for the family's loss. It couldn't have been easy to leave a beloved pet behind, and that made her doubly grateful she'd thought to give Miss Mischief — Comoară — to them yesterday.

Before she could express her sympathy, Donna Morgan of Bayside Souvenirs came hurrying up to speak to Mary.

"Good news, Mary," Donna said. "My friend who makes the little glass thingies to hang in windows brought me a whole box-ful to sell at the festival. I know they'll be popular."

"Excellent," Mary said. "Donna, I'd like you to meet some people who've recently moved to Sparrow Island." She quickly made the introductions and added, "They're from Romania."

"Well, welcome to —" The slender blonde's eyes popped wide open when she realized what Mary had said. "That's where Count Dracula lives," she said on a gasp of surprise.

Yousef appeared mildly amused by Donna's reaction. "The count is part of our history, yes."

"And all those vampires too!"

He shook his head. "Those are simply children's stories. You would call them old wives tales, yes?"

Flustered, Donna said, "Well, of course. I know they're just stories. But —" She backed a few steps away. "It was very nice to meet you all. I hope you'll be very happy here."

She glanced at Mary. "I have to run. I just remembered. I need to stop by the Green

Grocer in town and pick up some things for dinner."

As Donna fled toward the parking lot, Abby could only shake her head in amazement. Surely Donna would be the only resident of Sparrow Island anxious to protect herself from vampires because a family from Romania had moved here. What a silly superstition!

Still, there might be others who were prejudiced against newcomers, particularly foreigners who'd arrived so recently.

Abby vowed to help the Zekloses transition into the community as smoothly as possible. It was clear money was tight for them; Yousef couldn't be making much as a short-order cook.

An idea came to her, and she could barely wait until she and Mary got to the van before telling her.

"When I was at the cabin where the Zekloses are living, I discovered Ileana paints rocks she gathers on the beach like they were Easter eggs. They're beautiful. I'm sure people would be willing to pay good money for them as decorative pieces." She halted Mary's wheelchair beside the van. "I wonder if she'd like to sell some at your Best of Sparrow Island Festival."

Mary keyed the lift to lower. "That sounds

like a very good idea to me. They seem to be a lovely family, and I imagine they could use a little extra help settling in. I'll drop by to talk to her soon."

CHAPTER EIGHT

Sunday supper with the family after church had been a lifelong tradition for the Stantons. Despite her eighty years, Ellen continued to insist she prepare the Sabbath meal for her family.

Abby got down her mother's blue willow plates from the cupboard and set them on the table, which was covered with a bright floral cloth for the meal. There'd be six for supper today. Henry Cobb would be joining them as well as Sam Arbogast, their long-time farmhand who was a de facto member of the family.

While George Stanton was out in the barn consulting with Sam, Mary was busy at the butcher block counter in the kitchen that George had modified for her use. With practiced ease, she cut up apples to go in a spinach salad along with sliced almonds, mandarin orange sections and dried cranberries. Finnegan had found an out-of-the-way spot where he could lie down yet still be alert to Mary's needs.

She set her knife aside and scooped the apples into a large wooden salad bowl. "Mom, the next time you're at the Visitors Center would you ask if they'd like to have some brochures at the festival for tourists to pick up?"

"I'm sure they would, dear. But I'll ask." Opening the oven door, she pulled out the honey-basted ham that had been cooking and slid in a tray of buttermilk biscuits. A frilly apron protected the nice dress she'd worn to church. "Maybe I can bring them myself and answer questions."

"That'd be wonderful."

"Rick DeBow and I may be sharing the booth with you. We're going to put together some information on geocaching, and invite geocachers to drop by."

"That'll be nice. We'll have a chance to visit while we're there."

A quick rap on the back door, and Henry stepped inside. "Whatever you're having, I sure hope I'm invited to dinner. It smells terrific."

Laughing, Ellen welcomed Henry with open arms. "Of course you're invited."

Dressed in his uniform, he hugged Ellen then bent to kiss Mary's cheek. "Sorry I didn't make it to church. A toddler escaped his house this morning while his parents were sleeping late. We had one panicky mother on our hands."

"Did you find the child?" Mary asked.

"He hadn't gone far. He'd crawled into the neighbor's doghouse and gone back to sleep."

Mary placed her hand over her heart. "Thank the Lord!"

"What'd the dog think about being evicted from his house?" Abby asked.

"He wasn't evicted. The two of them were curled up together, comfy as a bug in a rug. The little boy apparently hadn't heard his mother calling him."

Chuckling, Abby imagined the dog sensed the child shouldn't be out on his own and intended to protect him as best he could. Animals were wise that way.

The cell phone at Abby's belt vibrated. That surprised her. She gave out her cell number to few people, most of whom were right there in the kitchen.

She pulled the phone from its holster and flipped it open. She didn't recognize the number.

"Who is it?" Mary asked.

"I don't know. Probably a wrong number." But something told her to answer anyway.

"Abby Stanton."

"Abby. It's Neil McDonald."

"Neil? Has something happened to Bobby?" They'd been planning to go fishing —

"No, we're fine. We're fishing right off the conservatory beach and there's some guy walking around acting really weird. It may be nothing, but I remembered you mentioning the fake IDs you'd found and . . ." — Abby could almost see Neil's shrug — ". . . I thought I should call. I'm sorry if I interrupted your supper."

The concerned attention of everyone in the kitchen was riveted on Abby as she listened to Neil.

"It's all right. I'm glad you called." She glanced at the others in the room. Whoever was behaving strangely was somewhere near the cache the young man had been searching for yesterday. A cache that shouldn't be there without the conservatory's permission. "I'll go check it out."

"You want me to stay here and keep an eye on the guy?" Neil asked.

"You should act natural. I don't want him spooked until I find out what's going on. It won't take me long to get there."

"We'll keep fishing. If you have any trouble, it'll take me two minutes to beach

134

the boat and get to you."

"Thanks, Neil. I'll let you know what happens."

She snapped the phone closed and returned it to its holster. Briefly, she explained what Neil had told her.

"I think I'd better see what's going on," she concluded.

"I'll go with you," Henry said.

"Your supper will get cold," Ellen warned.

"It's all right, Mom." Abby gave her mother a quick hug. "Cold ham will be fine. We shouldn't be long." She didn't really expect trouble, but she was grateful Henry had volunteered to come with her.

"Be careful, honey. You, too, Henry," Ellen said.

They went out the back door and both of them got into Henry's patrol car. It took only a few minutes to get to the conservatory parking lot, which was full of cars. There'd be plenty of visitors walking the trails, and Abby didn't want to put any of them at risk, which might happen if the stranger was involved in the counterfeit ID scheme.

"Maybe you should hang back a bit until I find out what's going on," Abby suggested as they got out the car. "There'd be less chance of the man becoming violent if he didn't spot your uniform right off."

"Abby, if there's *any* chance of violence, you shouldn't be here at all. I'll go in first." He touched his holstered weapon as though making sure it was there.

She scowled at him. "We'll go together, Henry. I know my way around the conservatory grounds better than you do, and I think I know what he's after."

Grudgingly, he agreed.

They hurried down the path toward the beach. They passed several families going in the same direction. Others were returning from the beach. All of them shot Abby and Henry curious looks, their haste drawing the attention of passersby.

Abby slowed when they reached the area the teenager had been searching yesterday. In almost the exact same spot a middle-aged man in khaki slacks and a tan windbreaker was pacing back and forth. He wore a white pith helmet and carried an open laptop in his arms.

"What's that sticking up out of his hat?" Henry asked under his breath.

As puzzled as Henry, Abby shook her head. "I have no idea."

"Let's find out."

Striding across the open ground, Henry

approached the stranger, Abby right behind him.

"Is there something we can help you with?" Henry asked when he was about five feet from the man.

The stranger started and snapped the computer closed. A couple of days' worth of whiskers darkened his cheeks and his eyebrows resembled a pair of fuzzy, black-and-gray caterpillars.

"Uh, nothing, officer. Just enjoying the outdoors. Getting some fresh air. Nice day, huh?"

Abby now saw that whatever was sticking up from the pith helmet was attached to the computer by a cord. She frowned, trying to figure out what the man was up to.

"You got a name?" Henry asked.

"Wendell. Wendell Jackson. Folks call me Dell."

"How 'bout an ID?"

Dell balanced his laptop with one hand and reached into his hip pocket for his wallet. "Am I doing something illegal?"

"I don't know," Henry said. "Are you?"

Abby finally got it. "You downloaded a topographical map to your laptop! And that thing on your hat is an antenna so you can pick up the satellite signal."

Surprised, Dell's gaze cut to Abby. "Yeah.

Nothing illegal about that as far as I know."

"Take your ID out of your wallet, please."

He tried to juggle the laptop while struggling to get his driver's license out of his wallet.

"Here, let me hold your computer." Abby took the laptop from Dell and stood next to him.

He managed to get his ID out and passed it to Henry. "What's this all about?"

"You're looking for a cache, aren't you?" Abby said. "Maybe I can help you."

"You're into geocaching too?"

Nodding, she opened his computer. "I'm also Associate Curator of the conservatory. No one asked permission to place a cache on the grounds, and I'd like to locate it myself."

"Well, it wasn't me," he said. "I've been here for thirty minutes and I can't find the fool thing. It's a tough one."

Her phone vibrated again. Removing it from the holster, she answered.

"Is everything okay?" Neil asked.

"We're good. Thanks," she replied.

"Okay. Bobby and I will move on up toward Paradise Cove. We haven't had a nibble here. Either the fish are too wily for us, or the tourists on the beach have been tossing rocks at them and chased them away."

She looked through the trees toward the water and spotted Neil's boat bobbing in the swells. "Good luck at the cove." Snapping the phone shut, she waved to her neighbor, then turned her attention back to Dell.

Henry returned the man's driver's license. "What brings you all the way from California to Sparrow Island, Mr. Jackson?"

"I've been in Bellingham the past two weeks on business. Pharmaceutical sales." He pulled a business card out of his wallet and handed it Henry. "Not much to do there on the weekends so I took the ferry over here this morning. I meant to bring my GPS with me, but I forgot to pack it. So I jerry-rigged this contraption."

"Let's see if I can figure out where the cache is hidden," Abby said.

She consulted with Dell and got the latitude and longitude coordinates, then studied the topographical map on the computer screen. "The cacher named this one Rock of Ages, so I'd guess whatever we're looking for is under a big rock."

"I figured that too," Dell said.

As Abby glanced around, however, she saw no obvious boulders, only an occasional fist-sized rock in the midst of the dry under-growth.

Shaking her head, she checked the topo-graphical map again. Ten feet from her loca-tion, the land dropped precipitously and then leveled again down to the beach. She tried to recall what was just beyond the line of trees. Geology wasn't her specialty but —

"I've got it," she announced.

"What have you got?" Henry asked.

"Ancient bedrock." Forgetting that the laptop she was holding was attached to Dell's hat, she started to walk toward the beach.

"Hey, wait." Dell hurried after her.

She grinned. "Sorry."

Only a few paces from where they'd been standing, but invisible from that location, lay a stretch of bedrock three feet high that had been exposed by the action of water over the centuries. She reached the spot, handed Dell the computer, jumped down and turned back to scan the denuded outcrop of bedrock. Not at all smoothed by time, there were dozens of nooks and cran-nies large enough to hold a cache.

Dell and Henry joined her, Dell squatting down so he could get a better look at the low wall of uneven rock.

"There," he said, pointing first then reaching his hand into a cavity not much bigger around than his arm. "Got it!" He stood, grinning, with a plastic container in his hand. "Man, I never would've found this baby. Thanks."

"You're welcome." HeeHaw, the cacher, had done a good job of hiding the cache, and Abby was as anxious as Dell to see the contents. So was Henry.

"What'd you get?" Henry asked.

Dell popped open the lid. "Logbook, chewed off pencil and a Vote for Nixon campaign button."

"Hey, that could be worth something," Henry commented. "Those antique shows on TV are always interested in political memorabilia."

"Guess it belongs to you." Dell offered the button to Abby. "You're the one who really found the cache."

"To tell you the truth, I'm more interested in finding out if there's anything else hidden in the hole." Kneeling, she looked and then reached inside. It wasn't very deep, and it was empty.

She glanced up at Henry and shook her head.

"What's going on here?" Dell asked. "You aren't just upset about this cache being hidden on conservatory property, are you?"

Henry took the lead in explaining the counterfeit ID scheme and what they'd be looking for, then apologized for hassling Dell.

"You thought I was an illegal alien or something?" He looked totally shocked by the prospect.

"We thought it was possible you could either be planting fake IDs or picking them up," Abby admitted.

Shaking his head, he denied the possibility. "I can get you a copy of my birth certificate, if you want. I was born in Santa Monica."

"No, I think you're clear with us," Henry said. "And I've got your address if we need to ask you any more questions."

Holding up the cache, Dell said, "What do you want me to do with this?"

"Go ahead and sign the log, then put it back." Abby knew others would come looking for it and the location caused no harm to the environment. It might even encourage others to visit and enjoy the conservatory grounds and stop by the Nature Museum. "But I am going to find out who HeeHaw is, if I can, and have a talk with him. He really should have gotten permission before planting the cache here."

Abby and Henry said good-bye to Dell

and walked back to his patrol car.

"Looks like it was just a false alarm," Abby said. "Sorry I dragged you away from Sunday supper."

"Don't worry about it. A lot of police work turns into a dead end. You just have to keep following leads until you get the answers you need."

Abby intended to do exactly that.

Abby was at her desk at the Nature Museum Monday morning when her cell phone rang. The caller was the owner of the geocaching Web site, Edgar Staples.

"I'm reluctant to give out personal information about our members," Staples said once Abby had explained the situation.

"I fully understand your position. However, someone appears to be using your Web site to either communicate information about a crime or to subvert the purpose of geocaching." She leaned forward as though she could be more persuasive if she could get closer to Edgar Staples. "Federal authorities have been notified and are trying to track down the source of the counterfeit IDs. I'm sure they'd appreciate your cooperation."

For a long moment, there was only silence at the other end of the line.

"If you're not willing to provide me with the information," Abby continued, trying to persuade Mr. Staples, "I can ask Agent Burns of Immigration and Customs Enforcement to call you, or our own Sergeant Henry Cobb of the sheriff's department. Or I'll give you their numbers and you can call them."

"You're really sure something's going on that's illegal?"

"Absolutely."

"I could insist you get a court order."

"Of course you could. But that would just delay things while the criminal activity continues. I don't think you want that, Mr. Staples."

Staples hesitated again, then sighed in defeat. "HeeHaw has been posting on the Web site for almost two years," he said. "I can't believe he's involved in anything illegal."

"If that's true, then he'd want to know someone messed with at least one of his caches. What's his real name, Mr. Staples?"

Again there was a long pause. "Melvin Reeves. He didn't give an actual address when he registered, only listed his home as Shaw Island in Washington."

Abby nodded to herself. She'd been sure HeeHaw lived locally, based on the number of caches he'd planted on the islands.

"I think I'll be able to find Mr. Reeves." Fewer than two hundred people lived on Shaw Island. A stop at the one small store on the island, or the post office, would lead her to HeeHaw and his whereabouts. "Thank you, Mr. Staples. You've been a big help."

"I hope I did the right thing by telling you about HeeHaw. I don't want to get sued."

Neither did she.

After disconnecting, she leaned back in her chair and stared at the poster above her desk, an eagle in flight. From all appearances, Melvin Reeves was a legitimate geocacher. There was no reason to suspect he was involved in the illegal scheme. But maybe because he was an experienced cacher he could have noticed unusual activity on the Web site or out in the field when he was planting a cache.

She glanced at her watch. She had some paperwork to catch up with, and tomorrow morning she intended to inventory sparrows in another section of the island. But her afternoon was free.

"No sense to put it off," she said aloud, picking up the photo of Davor Jovanovic that Agent Matt Burns had e-mailed her this morning. Perhaps Melvin Reeves would

145

recognize the man.

Mary found the dirt road to the cabins at Paradise Cove a bit bumpy for her van and there were still puddles in shaded spots from the last rain they'd had. She maneuvered around the worst of the mud until she reached the cabin where the Zeklos family was staying, their small car parked to the side. The uneven path up to the front porch didn't look very wheelchair friendly.

"Finnegan, it's possible I should have let Abby handle this errand." Switching off the engine, she released the catch that held her chair securely in place and freed Finnegan as well. She hadn't stopped to consider the cabin might not be accessible to her. "As long as we're here, we might as well give it a try."

She rode the lift down to the ground and wheeled onto the dirt. Finnegan tugged on his harness, helping her along. Within a few feet she hit a rut. The right wheel of her chair got caught.

"Well, for pity's sake," she muttered.

As she backed up a few inches, she noticed the curtain shift on one of the cabin's windows.

"Hello," she called. "Ileana, are you home?"

The curtain fell back into place, and a moment later Ileana opened the front door and hurried toward Mary. The young woman was wearing a knee-length smock, jeans and sandals.

"I heard your truck come and did not know who was here. I was afraid —" Ileana's words stopped abruptly. "Then I recognized you and your pretty dog. Can I help you?"

Stuck as she was, halfway between the van and the cabin, all Mary could do was laugh at her own foolishness.

"Why don't we talk right here for a moment, and I'll tell you why I've come. Then you can help me back to the van."

Although Ileana looked puzzled by Mary's request, she agreed. "Of course. If that is what you wish."

"Abby told me about the rocks you paint and how lovely they are."

A blush colored her cheeks. "It is only that I amuse myself while Yousef is at work. Caterina and I gather the rocks from the creek that runs into the cove. It is like a game to us."

"From what Abby described, I suspect you're being modest. She and I had an idea that you might want to make some extra money by selling your decorative rocks at our Best of Sparrow Island Festival."

Immediately, Ileana denied anyone would want to buy her rocks. But Mary persisted. When Ileana finally produced the plateful of ornately painted rocks, Mary was stunned. Selecting two, she studied the delicate designs on rocks that had been shaped and smoothed with the passage of time.

"Abby didn't exaggerate a bit. These are gorgeous!" Looking up at Ileana, she could tell the young woman was both pleased and embarrassed by her praise. "These are so exquisite, I believe you could sell them for a good price." She named a dollar figure that made Ileana's blue eyes widen in shock.

"That much?"

Mary laughed. "I know I'd be willing to pay that much, and I think I'd like to stock these rocks on consignment at my florist shop, particularly at Easter time."

As Mary continued to describe the festival, it was obvious Ileana was caught up in the idea of selling her rocks and earning a bit of extra money for the family. She thought in the next ten days she'd be able to paint more rocks in time for the festival. Because Caterina was attending Vacation Bible School, she had more spare time than usual to paint.

Still wide-eyed, Ileana said, "If I sold enough of my rocks, I could buy Caterina new shoes. She grows so fast."

"Growing's something children are very good at," Mary concurred. She recalled one summer when her son Zack outgrew every pair of pants and shoes in his closet.

She and Ileana discussed how many painted rocks would be appropriate for the festival and which designs might sell best. Finally, the details of how and when to deliver the rocks worked out, Ileana helped Mary maneuver her chair back to the van and gave her a grateful hug.

"Thank you for being my friend, Mary. In this new country I felt a stranger. And now I have you and your sister."

Mary gave her hand a squeeze. "When I had my accident, I learned the true value of friends and family. You can never have too many friends, and I'm more than pleased to count you among them. God bless you."

CHAPTER NINE

Abby saved time by skipping lunch at the office, deciding instead to pick up something to eat on the ferry to Shaw Island. After parking her car on the lower level, she headed directly upstairs to the main cabin and food service area. Except for two people selecting ready-made cold sandwiches, she was the first passenger to arrive. Yousef was working at the stove.

"Hello, Yousef. How are you this afternoon?"

He looked up and flashed her a quick smile. "I am well, thank you."

"How are your grilled cheese sandwiches today?"

His smile turned into a frown. "You would like my *sarmale* better, but regretfully that is not on the menu." He reached for two slices of bread and began buttering them.

"What's *sarmale?*"

"Ah, it is cabbage stuffed with rice and

meat with many good herbs and spices." He gestured, pinching his thumb and finger together, blowing a kiss in the air. "Very tasty. Perhaps someday I can show you good Romanian cooking."

"I'd like that very much. I'm always eager to try new foods."

She paid the cashier for the sandwich as well as a glass of iced tea. When her order was ready, she carried her tray to a table near the window so she could watch the passing scenery.

With little wind, the straits were calm and the sky was the same cloudless blue as her mother's willow plates. A few pleasure boats made their way toward Friday Harbor, their wakes folding vees through the water like an origami artist. A commercial fishing boat labored west toward the open sea.

She wondered if any of the boats she observed had individuals on board who lacked the papers needed to remain in America. Or could a skipper of one of the small boats that zipped by the ferry be planning to hide illegal documents under the ruse of being a geocacher? At the very least, it was a clever scheme. She imagined the culprit didn't expect to be caught.

And might not be, she realized. With the Immigration and Customs people overloaded with Homeland Security tasks, a few harmless illegals slipping across the northern border to make a better life for themselves could not be a high priority.

But if the illegal alien wasn't harmless? What then?

She'd finished her sandwich and tea by the time the loudspeaker announced the ferry's imminent arrival at Shaw Island. Until fairly recently, a group of Franciscan Sisters had run the ferry terminal and marina, and the nearby general store. Over the years the nuns in their brown habits became a landmark for visitors to the island. But with the passage of time, the four nuns aged and retired, and no others joined the order.

Abby was one of many who missed the nuns and the generous spirit they brought to their tasks.

When the ferry docked, she drove up the ramp onto solid land. She didn't have far to go before she pulled over at the general store. The clerk knew immediately who she was looking for.

"Oh sure. Ol' Mel lives out on West Sound," the young woman said. "His place is about two miles from here. An old log cabin with a satellite dish on the roof. Kinda hard to spot from the road. It's easier by boat if you've got one. He's got a nice dock and a twenty-one-foot Monaro. Can't miss it."

Abby thanked the woman and got back in her car.

Sparrow Island was pretty laid-back compared to Seattle or even to Bellingham. In contrast, Shaw Island was downright sleepy. Few people were on the street. A couple of pickups that would benefit from a makeover were parked in front of the post office. Not a lot of excitement going on today. Or any day, she suspected. Clearly the local residents preferred it that way.

With only two roads to choose from, Abby picked the one to West Sound.

Like children too shy to be seen, scattered houses hid in the pine and fir forest, sometimes only a mailbox alongside the road marking the presence of a nearby residence. An abundance of fireweed lined the side of the road with pink and purple blooms. Non-native rhododendrons and azaleas bloomed in profusion in front yards. Western hemlocks fought their way toward the sun in areas heavily shaded by the pines.

Through the trees, Abby spotted a log cabin well away from any other house. The faded name REEVES was on the mailbox, and she turned into the drive.

While she might regret the number of

trees that had been harvested to build the log cabin, she had to admit it looked cozy. A meandering thread of smoke rose from a chimney made of native stone; lichen covered the shaded side of the roof. When she reached the end of the drive, she was treated to a hundred-and-eighty-degree view of the sea spreading out in front of her with the profile of Lopez Island a three-dimensional cardboard cutout in the distance. Mr. Reeves's high-priced boat sat bobbing at his private dock.

Mr. Reeves himself appeared on his porch and waited for her to get out of her car. He had a long gray beard and his gray hair was pulled back in a ponytail.

"If you're a Realtor and want to sell my place, you might as well hop back in your car. You're wasting your time."

She sensed he didn't intend to be rude, simply forthright. Every Realtor in the county had probably lusted after this listing.

"If I had a view like yours, I wouldn't sell either, Mr. Reeves." She looked out toward Lopez Island once more before turning back to him and introducing herself, including her Associate Curator position at the Sparrow Island Nature Conservatory. "I'd like to ask you a few questions about the geocaches you've planted."

Surprise registered in his eyes. "How'd you find me?"

"I talked with the owner of the geocaching Web site. He very reluctantly shared your name with me, and only after I assured him that federal authorities were involved. If necessary, they'd be contacting him directly. When he understood the situation, he agreed it was important that I speak with you."

"Federal authorities?"

"That's right. Can we talk?"

Reeves hesitated a moment before inviting her up onto the porch to sit in one of two rustic armchairs made of manzanita wood. Green-and-white-striped cushions made out of awning material provided a comfortable seat.

"You folks at the conservatory upset about my planting a cache on your property?"

"It would have been better if you'd asked permission, which we would have given. But that's not why I'm here."

"Well, speak up, young lady. I quit trying to be a psychic when I retired from the stock market business. All that guessing where the next big merger or stock split would come lined my pockets with plenty of green, but it gave me the world's worst headache. Not worth it any more."

Though Mel Reeves appeared somewhat gruff, she didn't think he'd have reason to forge or plant fake IDs. Certainly not a financial motive. "How many caches have you hidden in the San Juan Islands?"

"Maybe twenty or so. I do it for kicks when I'm out fishing. You do any geocaching yourself?"

"Yes, a little. Have you noticed any of your caches being muggled lately?"

"Now that you mention it . . ." Thoughtfully, he tugged on his long gray whiskers. "Had that happen a couple of times recently. Both caches were on Sparrow Island."

"I'm probably the guilty party in one case." She told him about the cache she and Rick had found at Oyster Inlet, and what had been hidden beneath it.

"A forged green card? You think I'm trying to smuggle illegals into the country and give them fake IDs?" Clearly appalled by the idea, he shook his head. "No way, lady. It's high time we sealed our borders good and tight, I say."

"In any case, I'm hoping with all your experience geocaching that you can help me discover who's behind the scheme and how they're doing it." She handed him the picture of Davor Jovanovic that she'd brought along. "Do you recognize this man? Perhaps someone you've seen near one of your caches?"

Reeves studied the photo and slowly shook his head. "Never saw him before. Is he the illegal immigrant?"

"We think so, yes."

"You say the federal authorities are investigating the case?"

"They've agreed to look into it. But they're understaffed and our situation here doesn't appear to be a high priority for Immigration and Customs Enforcement."

Reeves stood abruptly. "Come inside. I'll show you my setup, and we can take a look at the other cache that's gone missing. See if anybody else is having trouble around here."

The inside of Reeves's cabin was compact and anything but rustic. A leather couch sat against one wall with an adjacent matching chair. The opposite wall had an array of electronic equipment including a state-of-the-art computer, printer, copier and two-way radios. Despite the satellite dish on the roof, there was no television in sight, and she guessed he accessed high-speed broadband Internet via the dish. A small kitchen was visible beyond a breakfast bar, and a doorway led to what Abby assumed would be a bedroom. The faint hint of wood smoke from the fireplace lingered in the air.

Everything in the room was neat and well organized.

Reeves dragged a stool from the breakfast bar and plopped it down beside the desk chair, which he took for himself.

Taking the hint, Abby perched herself on the stool. "Have you lived here long?"

At the touch of his hand on the computer mouse, the screen awakened. "Seven years." With a few key strokes, he brought up the geocaching Web site and the list of caches he'd planted.

Abby pointed at the screen. "Your 'Circle in the Pines' cache is where we found the fraudulent green card. Very clever hiding place, by the way."

"Thanks." He didn't take his eyes off the screen. "It's been out there since last summer. Got a few successful finds. Yesterday I got word the site got muggled. The guy wasn't too happy about it either."

Adjusting her glasses, she leaned forward. "Who posted that it was gone?"

"Guy named Seeker. That's his screen name anyway. I was planning to check the site in the next day or two. Replace the cache, if I had to."

Abby glanced at Reeves. Deeply tanned, his frown cut deep grooves across his forehead and there was a sunburst of crinkles at the corner of his eye from spending so much time outdoors.

"Why would Seeker say the site had been muggled instead of thinking he simply hadn't found it?" she asked.

He turned toward Abby. "Good question. I don't recognize Seeker as being from around here. Let's see if he's a regular."

Reeves did a search of the Web site. He found Seeker was a registered member, but there was no profile listed. The only comment he'd ever made about a cache was on the one at Oyster Inlet.

Leaning back, his eyes still on the screen, Reeves stroked his beard. "Either he's a novice at this hobby and it was his first time out, or he picked my cache for a good reason. He *expected* to find something more than my old Tupperware container."

"And by posting here, he's letting the person who promised him counterfeit IDs know that he didn't get them," Abby concluded. Seeker either was, or had intended to become, Davor Jovanovic. A shudder of unease rippled through her.

"Which is why he's so ticked off that the site was muggled."

"Right. So the next question is, how did he know to look there in the first place? How does the dealer communicate with the buyer and vice versa?" she reasoned out loud.

"You're one smart lady, Ms. Stanton. At least you know how to ask the right questions."

She rubbed her hand along the back of her neck and rotated her shoulders. "I may be smart, but I'm not a bit closer to finding out the source of the fake documents, or who the illegal immigrants are, than I was when I first found your cache."

"Maybe you're closer than you think. What you need to look for are individuals recently registered with the Web site who have only made one comment. That they found what they were looking for."

She felt a renewed spark of optimism. "Then I can get their names from the Web site owner and track them down."

"I don't think so." Shaking his head, he scrolled down through the caches that he'd listed. "Chances are good Seeker didn't leave his real name, and neither will anyone else who's buying a fake identity card. Probably buying a whole new identity, for that matter. But you should be able to connect the dots and come up with a pattern of which caches they're using."

"Wouldn't they use different hiding spots each time so they'd be harder to detect?"

"People are amazing creatures of habit. They've also got incredible egos, crooks and con artists in particular. Whoever's making and selling these fake IDs hasn't been caught yet. He figures he's so brilliant, nobody will ever find him out."

Reeves could well be right. He'd also come up with something concrete for Aaron to search for on the Web sites. It could increase their chances of getting a lead on the culprits.

"I've got to get back to the ferry landing or I'll miss the next departure and be late getting home." Standing, Abby extended her hand. "You've been very helpful. I appreciate your time." He took her hand in his, warm and slightly calloused, not like that of a stockbroker at all.

"It's nice for once to have an attractive woman drop by who doesn't want to sell my home out from under me."

She chuckled as he escorted her to the door.

"Maybe I'll stop by the conservatory again one day. To check on the cache I planted there," he added.

Looking up at him, she said, "Be sure to

visit the Nature Museum. We have some interesting displays I think you'd enjoy."

She held his gaze for a moment, wondering what he was thinking, then she walked down the steps from the porch to her car. Mel Reeves was an interesting man, going from stockbroker to outdoorsman, much like Rick DeBow.

Mel had also given her a new direction for her investigation. As soon as she got back to Green Harbor, she'd stop in at Holloway's Hardware to talk with Aaron. Surely they were on the right track now.

"By the way," she added as an afterthought. "We're going to have a geocaching event on Sparrow Island on Father's Day. It's part of the festival that's held at the Dorset, with a fish fry at the end of the day. If you're not busy that weekend, you might want to drop by."

His eyes crinkled with pleasure. "I'll put it on my calendar."

Mondays were rarely busy at Island Blooms.

After her visit with Ileana, Mary spent an hour or so at the shop, then decided she'd personally deliver this week's fresh floral arrangement to Little Flock while Candace handled anything else that might come up. The flowers were for her friend, Janet

Heinz, the church secretary at Little Flock, and she thought that even if she visited a few minutes, she'd still have time to fix dinner before she had to leave for her knitting group meeting. Some of the members were knitting baby sweaters and caps to be sold at the Best of Sparrow Island Festival.

The entrance to the church office was off to the side of the main chapel. When Mary pushed open the door, she heard Janet's radio playing one of her favorite hymns, "Here I am, Lord." She began to hum along as she and Finnegan went inside.

"Mary! You are indeed here." Janet, dressed in a lavender top with a flowing, moss-green skirt, came around from her side of the desk to take the floral arrangement. "It's good to see you."

"I thought I'd save Candace a trip out here to bring the flowers for your office." She gestured for Finnegan to sit.

"How sweet you are." Janet gave Mary a one-arm hug and placed the flowers on the corner of her desk. "So lovely. I look forward to a new bouquet every week, and every week the arrangement is lovelier than the last."

"Candace is very talented. She loves to try new combinations of whatever's in season." This week the mixed arrangement

163

included asters, ornamental poppies, cymbidiums and Boston ferns. They created a striking composition of color and textures.

Sitting down behind her desk, Janet set aside the papers she'd been working with. "Oh, I have to thank you and Abby for encouraging the Zekloses to enroll their little girl in Vacation Bible School. Caterina is such a dear little thing, and Ileana seems very sweet."

"Ileana is quite a talented artist too."

"They haven't lived here very long, have they? I don't recall seeing them around town." Janet was always on top of the pulse of the community, aware of the comings and goings of most of the residents.

"They've recently immigrated, I believe. The cabin they're renting at Paradise Cove is quite small. If they're going to stay here past the summer, they'll need someplace that's winterized better than where they are now."

"Perhaps later on, if they need a little extra help, Little Flock can step in to be of assistance. I'll mention to Rev. Hale that we have a new family in our congregation. He'll want to make a welcoming call to them."

"That would be wonderful. Ileana seems eager to make friends. It must be difficult to move to a country where you know no one at all."

Mary had never lived away from Sparrow Island and the friends she had here, except when she'd gone to college. The thought of leaving all she knew and moving to a foreign land where a different language was spoken would have given her more than a little pause. Yet the Zekloses had done just that.

What caused them to make such a drastic change? she thought.

Abby reached Holloway's Hardware shortly before closing time.

"Hey, Abby," Aaron said. "I was gonna call you this evening."

"Did you find something?"

"No, that's what I was gonna tell you." He straightened some flyers on the counter that advertised gasoline generators to be used during an emergency. "I've read all the posts I can find on three different geocaching Web sites and I've come up with zilch. I'm sorry —"

"It's all right," she interrupted. "I think I have a way for you to identify the people who're buying the fake IDs, and from that we should be able to tell which caches they're using." She told him about her visit with Mel Reeves and his suggestion for searching the Web sites. "Do you think that'd work?"

Scratching his head, then finger combing his hair back from his forehead, Aaron nodded. "I think so. I'll get on it tonight, and we'll hope for the best."

CHAPTER TEN

Shortly after dawn on Tuesday morning, Abby drove to Cedar Grove Lake. The freshwater lake near the center of Sparrow Island provided good fishing and swimming during the summer months. But at this hour of the day the quiet was broken only by the call of birds and the hum of insects.

She parked near a meadow carpeted by tall grass, the landscape a variegated green accented with bright spots of colorful wildflowers. A perfect habitat for Savannah sparrows and possibly Vesper sparrows.

Wearing her birding vest and carrying her clipboard, she started out across the field she planned to survey. Long blades of grass whispered against her jeans as she walked; her hiking boots left a visible trail where she'd crushed the grass underfoot. The scent of rich, damp soil and an earthy perfume rose with each step.

Last night she'd checked the geocaching

Web site for caches in this area. There were none listed. Oddly, almost all of the caches on the island were most easily accessed by boat, not car.

Abby wondered if that meant both the copycat cacher and the illegal aliens arrived by boat on Sparrow Island. If so, who was providing the boat? And where were they coming from?

In terms of the immigrants, Canada seemed the most logical answer, specifically Vancouver Island, which was less than thirty miles away. She wondered if they had been in Canada legally, using that country as a way point before entering the United States. Or perhaps they had a visa to be in the United States as a tourist and the fake IDs would allow them to stay indefinitely.

Did that mean the forger was already in the States? Perhaps a US citizen who covered his tracks and his illegal activities by using a geocaching Web site?

She was deep in thought when a demure Savannah sparrow rose from a clump of grass with a *tseep* and fluttered off to Abby's right, immediately becoming invisible again in the tall grass. She noted the sighting on her diagram and walked on.

From the corner of her eye, Abby caught the quick dive of a kingfisher just before he entered the lake with a splash. She turned in time to see the shaggy-headed bird rise from the water with a small fish in his beak and take flight for his perch on top of a tall fir on the opposite shore, his early morning angling excursion successful.

At a leisurely pace, she crisscrossed the meadow, identifying more Vesper and Savannah sparrow activity and recording the information for later input at the Nature Center.

By the time she finished the survey, her jeans had attracted all manner of burrs and seeds, and the ridged soles of her boots were packed with mud. At the car, she changed into street shoes, dropping the muddied boots on a newspaper in the trunk. The burrs she picked off as best she could.

She loved that her job allowed her to be outside among all the glories God had created, but admitted there were some small inconveniences that went along with the blessings.

Skirting the main part of town, Abby arrived at the Nature Museum and parked her car. She fell in behind a family of visitors as they walked toward the stucco-and-stone building. She smiled as the little girl, who was about four years old, skipped up the steps flapping her arms.

"Look, Mommy! I'm a bird and I can fly!"

"Yes, dear. I see that. But be sure you perch right next to me in the museum so I don't lose you."

The family followed the arrows on the floor toward the first display, a bald eagle with a fish clutched in his talons. The little girl squealed in delight.

As laughter tickled her throat, Abby greeted Wilma, who was behind the reception counter.

"I'd say we have a budding ornithologist in our midst," she said.

"I'm convinced the museum's exhibits and the guided tours cause a lot of youngsters to consider wildlife careers. At least for the few hours they visit us."

"If they come away from the experience with an appreciation of nature and a respect for the environment, we've done our job." She started for the doorway to the office area, then stopped. "Did you find out anything about that woman who sent the three baskets from Friday Harbor?"

Shifting her long, gray hair behind her shoulder, Wilma shook her head. "You know, not a soul in the tribe knows who she is. Her name's Ashley Tomlins, which doesn't sound like a Lummi tribal name at all. Or from any other tribe, for that matter."

"Perhaps that's her married name."

"That's possible. At any rate, I'm going to have to duck away early one afternoon this week and see what I can find out."

"Well, I hope she's not trying to slip a phony basket past you, claiming it's Native-made."

Wilma agreed, and Abby continued on to her office, dropping her clipboard on her walnut desk before putting her purse away in the bottom drawer. Sitting down, she turned to her computer and brought up her sparrow inventory report. Doing data entry wasn't her favorite part of her job, but the results of surveys such as this one provided a way to see the trends in wildlife population and provide an early warning system if populations declined precipitously. Knowledge would allow her and others to get to the root causes of a problem.

She'd been working about an hour when Aaron Holloway burst into her office. Dressed for work, he had on khaki wash pants and a cotton sport shirt.

"I've got it! I found which caches they're using!" Grinning broadly, his dark eyes bright with excitement, he handed her several sheets of computer printouts. "Your friend over on Shaw knew what he was talking about."

"That's wonderful!" His enthusiasm contagious, Abby quickly scanned the sheets of paper, then shook her head. "What am I supposed to be looking at?"

He dragged a chair around to sit next to her. "Look at these entries." He grabbed a yellow highlighter from her desk and stroked the felt tip across the page once and did the same on the next two pages. He marked a total of six entries. "Each of those entries was made by a guy who never before or after found another cache or hid one himself. Two times it's the cache at Oyster Inlet you found with the fake IDs. Three times it's a cache out by Wayfarer Point Lighthouse. And once the posting was for a location at Paradise Cove."

This time, adjusting her glasses, she studied each posting more carefully, noting the dates the caches had been found and how long they'd been hidden. "So you're saying over the past two to three months there've been at least six sets of counterfeit IDs picked up here on Sparrow Island." The possibility of so much illegal activity in such a short period stunned her.

"Not necessarily. One or more of these cache finds could be coincidence. It just happened that some guy found a cache, got bored with the idea of treasure hunting, and didn't ever try again. But they can't all be pure coincidence. None of the other caches we've got on the island have been found by first-timers who didn't post again."

"Interesting." She pondered what they should do next. "Is it possible to trace back the entries under the various screen names and find out who originated the message?"

"Maybe. Every computer has a unique Internet provider number. It's like a home address. Basically, anyone can find it if they know where to look."

"That sounds a lot like Big Brother is watching," she commented.

"In a way, it's exactly like that. But we can use that to our advantage if the Internet service provider will give us the number they assigned to the subscriber of their service. From that, if we can get payment information, we can trace it back to Seeker and MidLife and the other solo screen name entries."

"I'm beginning to think that what I don't know about computers and the Internet would fill an entire library."

He grinned at her again. "That's how come I spend so much time reading."

"Well, you've certainly soaked up a great

deal of information. Now the question is, what do we do with this?" She tapped the printed sheets with the tip of her finger.

"I can keep working on it. See how far I can get."

Nervous about poking into the private e-mails of people who could be entirely innocent, Abby hesitated. Still, she didn't want to miss the chance to stop the criminal activity if she could.

"I think we need to talk to Sergeant Cobb before we take the next step on our own," she said. "He may want to consult with Matt Burns, the immigration agent, so we don't jeopardize a criminal case, if it comes to that."

"Okay." Still eager, Aaron appeared thoroughly committed to getting to the bottom of the case. "When do you wanna go see him?"

She smiled to herself. "Let me finish some of this data entry, and then we can be on our way."

Before Abby and Aaron left the museum, she called the sheriff's substation and discovered Henry was having lunch with Mary at the Springhouse Café. Given Aaron's need to get back to work at the hardware store within a reasonable amount

174

of time, she hoped her sister and the sergeant wouldn't mind if they made it a foursome.

Located on Shoreline Drive, Springhouse Café provided diners with an unobstructed view of Randolph Bay and the marina. The menu was varied and moderately priced, making the restaurant popular with both islanders and tourists.

Together, Abby and Aaron walked up the steps to the entrance and passed through the café's gift shop, coming to a halt at the hostess podium. Ida Tolliver greeted them. A slender blonde about Aaron's age, she filled in part-time as a receptionist at the Nature Center and often volunteered more hours to help Abby with bird walks.

"Hi, Abby." Ida flashed a grin in Aaron's direction as she picked up a couple menus. She wore the café's standard waitress uniform of navy pants, white blouse and an apron. "You two together?"

Aaron shifted uncomfortably on his feet. "Yeah, I guess," he mumbled, his gaze sliding away from the attractive waitress.

Abby spotted her sister and Henry sitting at a window table. "Actually, we'd like to join Mary and Henry, if we can."

Ida glanced over her shoulder. "Sure. That'll work."

She set off at a quick pace, Abby following, Aaron tagging along behind. Abby suspected that Aaron had a crush on Ida, but was too shy to do anything about it.

Bright tablecloths in a cabbage rose print lent a cheerful note to the café's friendly ambience as did the matching window drapes, which were tied back so the patrons could enjoy the view. A busy lunch crowd filled most of the tables and there was a pleasant hum of conversation.

"I've brought you company." Ida set the menus on the table in front of the two vacant seats.

"Well, hello there," Mary said, gesturing for Finnegan to shift his position to make room for the new arrivals.

Henry half stood at his seat. "Glad to have you. We just ordered, so you haven't missed out."

"I'll take your orders right away if you know what you want," Ida said. "And I'll see that they come up at the same time as Mary and Henry's."

Abby took the chair next to her sister. "That'd be very nice, Ida. Thank you." Familiar with the menu, she ordered a Cobb salad and iced tea.

Sitting next to Henry, Aaron ordered a cheeseburger, fries and a Coke without ever once looking up at Ida.

"You got it, hon," she said cheerfully.

Adjusting her place setting, Abby said, "I hope you two don't mind us barging in on you."

Mary patted her hand. "Of course not. I was running some errands in town and there was Henry right behind me at the Green Grocer checkout line. So he invited me to lunch. Purely a coincidence that we met."

"Truth is, Mary, I spotted your van. Decided to take advantage of the situation and tracked you down on the off chance you didn't have a date for lunch."

Her cheeks coloring slightly, Mary shared a fond look with the sergeant. "I'm flattered."

"At the risk of interrupting such a romantic moment," Abby teased, "Aaron has come up with some important information about which caches the counterfeiters are using for a drop to hide their fake IDs."

That got Henry's full attention. He accepted the computer printout from Aaron and listened attentively to the explanation of what had been discovered. He barely glanced up when Ida brought the drinks, or even when she brought their orders, concentrating instead on understanding the complexities of Internet service providers and tracking down subscribers.

Both Abby and Mary ate their salads while paying close attention to Aaron's explanation.

Henry finally took a couple of bites of his tuna salad sandwich and a sip of iced tea. "This is good information, Aaron. I'm impressed."

The younger man looked pleased with Henry's praise. "Once I got onto what I had to search for, it was pretty easy to identify the individual postings on the Web site."

"We thought we'd better let you know what he'd found before we went any further trying to track down the people involved," Abby said.

Nodding, Henry finished the first half of his sandwich and another swallow of tea. "You did the right thing bringing this information to me. To keep things legal, I think Agent Burns will have to get a federal search warrant before we do anything else."

"How long will that take?" Mary asked.

He shook his head. "I don't know. He'll have to get his computer expert to check out what Aaron's discovered. Then they'll have to build a case based on probable cause."

"But won't he be able to move a little

faster now that we have a solid lead?" Abby asked.

"You'd think so," Henry agreed. "But the wheels of government run slow when a bureaucracy as big as Homeland Security's involved. Immigrant and Customs Enforcement is only one cog in that cumbersome circle of agencies."

Discouraged, Abby sighed. "Isn't there anything we can do to speed things up?"

Aaron spoke up. "We could post someone at each of these likely cache sites and have them watch for any activity, then nab whoever shows up."

"Easier said than done, son. I don't have anywhere near the manpower necessary to watch those locations twenty-four hours a day. And who knows when, or even if, someone would try to plant another set of papers."

"Someone should at least check those sites now to see if there's already something hidden there," Mary suggested.

"I can do that." Abby toyed with the few remaining bites of cheese in her salad. "I'm sure Rick DeBow will go with me again. But I'm thinking . . ."

They all looked at her expectantly.

"Years ago, while I was still an undergraduate, I was involved in a study to identify how many pine martens — that's a small species of weasel — were active in the Stanislaus forest in northern California. They're very illusive creatures and hunt mostly at night."

"I remember that," Mary said. "You had a summer internship with some nonprofit environmental group. Mom was scared to death you'd be attacked by a mountain lion or something."

Abby chuckled. "Fortunately, that didn't happen. But we did catch a female marten with two of her kits on film."

"Wow! Neat stuff," Aaron said.

"How'd you do that?" Henry asked.

"We set out some bait for the marten along a path she was likely to travel. Then we set up a motion detection camera and used an infrared beam. When the marten broke the beam, the camera was triggered to take a picture."

"Clever idea." Aaron did a thumbs-up.

"We were successful. Although in the process of getting a couple of good shots of pine martens, we lost a camera to an angry brown bear that didn't like having his picture taken. And we wasted a lot of film on smaller animals like foxes, who apparently liked the idea of a free meal too."

Henry tugged thoughtfully on his uniform

shirt collar, smoothing the tips. "That might work, Abby. But assuming we had some infrared equipment — which I don't — the suspect is likely to spot the beam and figure out what's going on. Chances are good he'd take the camera and toss it somewhere. He'd sure destroy the film."

That dampened Abby's excitement, and she tried to think of an alternative.

"I know what we can use," Aaron said. "A motion-activated nanny cam. Lots of families that have full-time or live-in babysitters use them. I had a salesman drop by just a week or so ago. I didn't order any of the nanny cams. They're pretty expensive for our customer base. But I'm sure I've still got his card."

Henry jerked his head toward Aaron. "This kid knows about subjects that sure weren't covered when I went through the police academy. Now the problem will be getting the county sheriff to approve spending the money to buy a couple of nanny cams. They're not exactly in the budget."

"I'll get 'em on loan." On a roll now, Aaron became animated. "The salesman offered to do that to get some buzz going. The cameras can be remotely monitored and recorded. We'll have a complete video record of whoever shows up near the caches and what they do."

"That sounds perfect to me," Mary said.

"How soon do you think the salesman could get the equipment to us?" Henry asked.

"I figure by Thursday or Friday at the latest. The guy was really anxious to develop a market here."

Excited by the prospect of catching the culprit, Abby said, "I'll see if Rick and his GPS are available for a little treasure hunting trip tomorrow. When we find the caches, I'll have a chance to plan where to hide the camera."

Folding the computer printout, Henry tucked it in his inside jacket pocket. "I think we've got a plan, folks. I'll talk to Agent Burns, let him know what we're up to and ask him to expedite the search warrant, if that's what he needs."

They discussed the plan for a few more minutes, then Abby said, "By any chance, Henry, were any of your men able to identify the man's picture on the fake IDs we found?"

"Nope. Not yet. They've all got copies, though, and are keeping an eye out for the suspect."

"What picture's that?" Aaron asked.

Henry produced the photo from his

pocket. "Davor Jovanovic, according to his ID. Born in Croatia. He's supposed to reside in Seattle, only the street address is phony."

Studying the picture, Aaron shook his head. "Doesn't look familiar to me."

Just then Ida returned to the table. "Want me to take your plates now?"

Not a speck of food was left on Aaron's plate, so she picked his up. Abby indicated she was through as well.

Aaron held up the photo. "Ida, you ever see this guy in here?"

Still holding the empty dishes, she tilted her head to look at the stranger's picture. "He looks kinda familiar, you know, like I served him sometime. But we get a lot of folks in here and sometimes . . ." She shrugged sheepishly. "I don't always pay much attention to what they look like, just mostly worry about what they order, you know?"

"That's understandable," Mary said.

Ida reached across the table to pick up Mary's plate, then stopped. She looked back at the photo, then took it from Aaron. "You know, I do remember this guy. He came in for lunch one day last week. I think it was Friday. I remember him now 'cuz he seemed upset about something. His English wasn't real good and he got ticked off when I had

183

trouble understanding him."

Henry leaned forward. "Was anyone with him?"

"No. I'm pretty sure he was alone." She handed the picture back to Aaron.

"I don't suppose he used a credit card, did he?" Henry asked.

"No, paid cash. Decent tip, but not enough to write home about."

"This is important, Ida," Abby said. "Do you know if he'd arrived by ferry, or did he have a boat in the marina?"

"Oh golly, I'm not sure." Her blonde eyebrows pulled together as she tried to remember. "He was wearing a dark polo shirt, navy blue, I think. One with the logo of Butchart Gardens on the pocket."

"The one in Victoria, British Columbia?" Abby asked.

"Yeah, that's the place. I noticed 'cuz he didn't seem the type to visit a touristy spot like that. He was more, I don't know, rough around the edges." She glanced at the tables she was serving. "Look, I gotta get hopping. If I think of anything else about the guy, I'll let you know." She scurried off to the next table, promising the customer she'd be right back with a refill of coffee.

Aaron shook the remains of the ice cubes in his Coke glass and drank the liquid

184

down. "Seeker posted a message on Friday afternoon that the site he'd been looking for was muggled."

"That was the site Mel Reeves planted at Oyster Inlet," Abby told them. "The one where we found the fake IDs."

They all remained silent contemplating what they had just learned.

"I'm going to have my men ask some questions around the marina," Henry said. "See if anyone spotted this guy on the docks, maybe where the transient boats tie up. We'll take a whack at the ferry crews, too, but I think that's a long shot."

Abby knew what she'd be doing tomorrow morning — checking out the cache sites Aaron had identified as possible mail drops for the false IDs. She prayed they'd soon get a lead they could track back to the counterfeiting ring itself and the criminals who were running it.

All in God's time, she reminded herself.

CHAPTER ELEVEN

Wayfarer point jutted into the straits on the northern tip of Sparrow Island like an extra appendage stuck on the island as an afterthought. A lighthouse stood at attention on the rugged spit of land to warn passing ships of the rocky promontory. Accessible by road from Green Harbor, the windswept location was a popular destination for picnickers and sightseers, although no early morning tourists had ventured out this direction so far today.

Abby bent to pick up a plastic grocery bag that had been left to blow around the area. A curious sea gull could easily be snared by the innocuous bit of plastic and die of either strangulation or starvation.

Beside her, Rick DeBow studied his GPS unit. "According to Midlife's posting on the Web site, the cache has a view of the sea."

"Considering all of Wayfarer Point has a sea view, that's not real helpful."

She started across the sun-bleached land-scape toward the lighthouse, which rose forty feet above the sea, its light faithfully signaling danger every few seconds. Waves rolled ashore with hypnotic regularity, tumbling the rocks like a sculptor turns clay, smoothing the edges until they were round. Twenty feet from the shore where the waves broke, a line of spray lifted into the air and rainbows danced in the sunlight only to fall into the sea again. The song of stone and water became God's joyous melody of creation.

"If the cacher hid his cache under a rock, we're going to have fun turning over every stone on the beach," Rick commented.

"Let's hope it doesn't come to that."

"There's no way to get inside the light-house, is there?"

"No, it should be locked up tight. The Coast Guard automated the light years ago and let the lighthouse keeper go." The small whitewashed house that squatted next to the tower had been abandoned and boarded up for so long that Abby couldn't remember when it had last been occupied.

"Too bad. Bet it's a terrific view from up top." He angled his footsteps to the far side of the lighthouse. Like Abby, he was wear-ing hiking boots, jeans and a lightweight jacket over a sweater. "According to this, the GPS coordinates are on the north side of the lighthouse."

As they rounded the side of the building, the breeze caught Abby's hair, blowing it into her eyes. She held the strands back with her hand, thinking it might be time to get a haircut.

Keeping their eyes on the ground, they examined the area near the structure, looking for a spot where a small box might be hidden. At the next corner, Abby stopped.

"Cachers sure don't make their sites easy to find," she said.

"That's what makes it fun. The challenge." Rick stepped a few feet away from the lighthouse, his gaze scanning the whitewashed wall. He pointed. "Try there."

Right behind Abby was what looked like a metal fuse box. She tugged on the latch. It popped open easily, revealing a plastic first aid kit. The power lines that formerly brought electricity to the lighthouse had been removed, leaving only a hole for the conduit.

"This has to be it." Inside the box she found a logbook, stubby pencil and a child's barrette. No illegal documents.

Rick joined her. "Okay, we found the cache. But there's not enough space in here to hide one of those metal tubes we found at Oyster Inlet. Assuming this is one of the caches the counterfeiter's using, there has to be something more."

"Maybe there's another hidey-hole nearby." She glanced around but nothing popped out at her.

"At the other cache, the fake documents were hidden behind the legitimate cache." Taking hold of the fuse box, he tugged. Without much effort, the box slid out. Behind it were wooden studs and plenty of room to hide something else.

"Looks like this could be our spot." Abby looked around again, trying to think how she could set up a camera and disguise it so it wouldn't be noticed by the culprit they were trying to catch or stumbled upon by a tourist who might remove it. The area was open to the tree line about thirty feet away.

Rick followed her gaze. "That's a long way to get a picture clear enough to identify our suspect. And a lot of folks come out here to picnic. They'd be setting off the nanny cam when they weren't anywhere near the cache."

"You're right. But there has to be some way . . ." Looking up, she noticed that a narrow overhang circled the lighthouse about fifteen feet off the ground. Probably something to do with the structure's stability. "What if we mounted our camera up there? It'd look like something the Coast Guard had installed for general security purposes."

He considered her idea, looking at the spot from several angles and finally nodding his approval. "I think that's the best we can do. If we offset the camera a bit, not have it right overhead, and use a wide-angle lens, we'd get a decent shot. I've got an extension ladder at the marina we can use."

"Then the only question is will we be able to monitor the nanny cam from my home or office?"

"We'll have to test it to make sure. If it won't transmit that far, maybe we can use a satellite connection."

"Great. Meanwhile, we'll hope the Coast Guard doesn't come out here to inspect the lighthouse while our camera is stuck up there. They might take exception to what we're doing."

Rick grimaced and shoved the fuse box back into place. "Defacing government property can't involve too much jail time, do you think?"

Laughing, she headed back to the end of the road where Rick had parked his truck. Since they were already familiar with the cache site at Oyster Inlet, that meant they only had to visit and find the third possible mail drop that Aaron had identified — the one at Paradise Cove.

Mary wheeled her way up to the entrance of the Dorset in ample time for her Wednesday morning meeting with the Best of Sparrow Island committee. Her part of rounding up exhibitors was going well, and she hoped the others were having equal success.

She noticed the two young gardeners from Belize were at work again this morning. One was trimming a hedge while the other looked on, a rake in his hands. From the amount of debris on the ground, it didn't appear the designated raker was keeping up with his part of the job. But perhaps he was waiting for his partner to finish and get out of the way before he started.

With Finnegan leading the way, she greeted Muldoon, who held open the door for her. She rolled past the reception desk where a well-dressed couple appeared to be checking out.

Before she reached the library, the young man from Belize she'd met on her last visit appeared carrying a tray.

"Good morning, ma'am. Nice to have you and your dog visit the Dorset again." His housekeeping staff uniform was neatly pressed, his hair cut short and tidy.

"Thank you, Damani. How's your job coming along?"

"I like it very much, ma'am. I've brought some cookies for your meeting. They've lovely little bits of jelly in the middle."

"You're determined to tempt me to eat sweets, aren't you?"

He flashed her a beautiful smile. "I'm sure Mr. Gordon would say that's part of my job, ma'am."

He stood back to allow her to enter the library first, then discretely placed the tray of cookies on the long table next to the tea and coffee service. He nodded to Keith Gordon as he left.

The only other member of the committee who had arrived so far was Ana Dominguez. Mary greeted her friend as well as Keith.

"That Damani's a delightful young man," she said. Unable to resist, she plucked a cookie from the tray.

"He's been a real find." Keith poured a cup of tea for Mary and slid it across the table to her. "Pleasant disposition and willing to do anything we ask of him. I could use another half dozen just like him."

The rest of the committee arrived in short order. Artie Washburn was in his uniform and took his usual seat. Brenda Wilson, who was wearing a nice pair of khaki pants and a cotton blouse, had apparently skipped her fishing expedition this morning.

Donna Morgan rushed in last, breathless as though she'd been running. She dropped heavily into the nearest chair. "Sorry to be late. My aunt called from Spokane. It was so nice to talk to her, I just couldn't pull myself away."

Keith cleared his throat. "Why don't we get started."

Artie reported that his Aunt Wilma was checking the authenticity of some of the baskets she'd received, but other than that, everything seemed to be moving along fine.

"The entries for the Bass Fishing Classic are going pretty slow," Brenda said. "Not many father-son teams have signed up, and the sea bass that've been caught are smaller than I'd hoped. Biggest one we've weighed was just over two pounds."

"Maybe we should make sure folks know that father-daughter teams can enter too," Ana suggested.

"Oh, sure. That's on all the flyers." Brenda reached for a second cookie. "In fact, the pair with the biggest fish so far is a dad and his ten-year-old girl. She's a real fisherman, that little gal."

Mary wondered how Bobby and his father were doing. Apparently they weren't in first place so far. But there were ten days left in the contest. She couldn't help but hope her young neighbor came out on top.

"We have one additional participant for the festival," Mary reported. "Abby and Rick DeBow are arranging a geocaching event on Sunday afternoon. They'll share space with the Visitors Center."

"I don't understand." Confusion shaded Ana's dark eyes. "Abby's going to have a geo-what-event?"

Chuckling, Mary tried to explain the latest treasure hunting craze. "Not that I'm an expert, you understand. Mostly it seems to be an excuse to be outdoors," she concluded.

When the meeting was over, Keith walked Mary out. Finnegan assisted her the rest of the way to her van, and she headed into town to stop by Island Blooms for a few minutes on her way home.

The Geocache at Paradise Cove had been posted by someone who called himself Baldy. He had named the site Dive In.

Standing on the south side of the cove, Abby looked across the way at the cabin the Zekloses were renting, which was barely visible through the trees. There was no boat tied up at the rickety dock that went with the cabin, not that she expected Yousef to own a boat. Their financial situation seemed too tight for any extras.

Holding his GPS in his palm, Rick strolled toward one of the newer docks on this side of the cove. It belonged to Stuart Lynch and his family, old friends of Abby's parents who had owned a cabin here for years. The Lynches didn't often visit these days, although they still kept a small powerboat in the adjacent boathouse for use by their adult children and grandchildren when they brought their families to the island for a vacation.

"I hope we don't have to get wet to find this one. If it's at the bottom of a piling, we're in trouble," Rick said.

"I'm not sure I have access to an underwater camera, so let's hope the cache is above the tide line." The floating dock flexed under Abby's feet as she followed Rick.

Kneeling, he peered over the end of the dock. "Got it." He squatted back on the dock and showed her a Styrofoam box that looked like it might have been used originally to pack frozen food. He pried the lid off. "No fake IDs here."

"Is there a spot behind that box where

something else could be hidden?"

Setting the Styrofoam box aside, he peered over the side again. "Maybe on a crosspiece that's under here," he said, his voice muffled. "You'd sure have to know where to look."

That was just the kind of hiding spot the counterfeiter needed.

Glancing around, Abby tried to plan where to hide a camera that would be activated by movement at the end of the dock.

"Can I help you folks with something?"

Abby whirled to find a stranger approaching from the direction of a neighboring cabin. Taller than six feet, he had massive shoulders and arms that strained the seams of his T-shirt, delineating well-toned pecs and biceps.

"No, we're fine. We're friends of the Lynches, who own this cabin and the dock." Abby responded cautiously, not wanting to give away too much but eager to find out who this man was. "Are you renting one of the cabins?"

His gaze swung to Rick, who'd come to his feet. At five feet seven, he'd be no match for this giant, if the stranger was looking for a fight.

"Yep. Been here a couple of weeks," the

man said, shifting his attention back to Abby and eyeing her suspiciously. "It's early in the season and there're not many folks around. Except at this here dock. It's been real popular lately."

"Really?" Abby wondered if he might have seen the person who was planting the forged IDs.

As casual as can be, Rick strolled over to the stranger. "Maybe they're geocachers like we are."

The stranger's brows slammed into a straight line. "Geo-who?"

"Let me show you." Gesturing for the stranger to follow him, Rick walked back out to the end of the dock explaining geo-caching as he went. Then he pointed out the cache under the dock and demonstrated his GPS device.

The stranger sat back on his haunches and relaxed, no longer intimidating. "So that's what all the activity's been about. I thought maybe somebody was hiding drugs or dope here, something like that."

"We hope not." Abby joined the two men. "Can you describe the people you've seen here? Maybe we know them."

"Let me think." He stood, towering over Abby again. "The first guy I saw here was the day we arrived. A bald fella wearing a fishing hat. Then there was a good-lookin' black kid, maybe twenty years old." He ran his palm across his cheek that showed a day's worth of whiskers. "Then another guy showed up a couple of days ago. Kind of skittish acting and wearing a hooded sweatshirt. He's the one that made me nervous. But I didn't get a real good look at him."

Baldy had been the screen name of the one to originally plant the cache, the first person the stranger had seen here, Abby assumed. As for a young black man, there weren't many African Americans living on Sparrow Island, but Mary had mentioned meeting a summer hire at the Dorset who fit that description. As for the nervous visitor, that could have been anyone, including an illegal alien picking up IDs he'd bought and paid for.

After a bit more conversation about how to get into geocaching, the stranger wished them a good day and strolled back to his cabin.

Abby exhaled in relief. "Just the size of that man frightened me. But he didn't seem to faze you. How come?" she asked Rick.

He shrugged. "I figured a man built like that knows he doesn't have to get into fights to win. In fact, he loses if he starts swinging because he'll get sued if anyone's hurt. So I decided to be mostly straight with what we were doing."

"I'm glad you did. Maybe now we have a description of who's been planting the counterfeit documents."

"Or maybe just a description of a couple of innocent geocachers who located this cache."

Conceding that was true, Abby decided she could hide the camera under the eaves of the Lynches' boathouse. It would be inconspicuous, yet still close enough to the dock to get a good shot of any visitors who came looking for the cache.

Now all she needed was the salesman to provide Aaron with the cameras on loan, get them installed, and they'd be set to identify the crook. Assuming he planted another set of phony IDs at one of the three cache sites.

CHAPTER TWELVE

The following morning, Abby led a group of twenty day camp kids from Friday Harbor on a birding hike up to Arrowhead Hill. She split the fifth and sixth graders into four teams and engaged them in the process by letting them spot birds themselves and identify them based on the handouts she'd provided. They performed amazingly well, competition spurring them on.

Even so, she was tired when she returned to the museum. Teachers who spent an entire day, every day, with energetic eleven- and twelve-year-olds had her admiration.

Wilma was behind the counter when Abby entered the building.

"How'd it go?" Wilma asked.

"Quite well, if a bit exhausting. There were a couple of really sharp youngsters in the group." She'd gratefully handed off the students and their counselors to a pair of the conservatory docents for a guided tour of the grounds.

"Glad to hear it." Stepping out from behind the counter, Wilma straightened a display of birding maps that marked nesting sites on the island where bald eagles were most likely to be seen. The maps also carried a warning not to get too close to the nests to avoid disturbing young hatchlings and their parents.

"Did you ever find out whether those baskets were Native made?"

"Oh yes, I meant to tell you first thing this morning." Wilma's dark eyes sparkled with her news. "Turns out Ashley Tomlins is only fifteen years old. She's the daughter of a Lummi woman who died when Ashley was two years old. She lives with her dad and stepmother, who are both Anglo and know very little about Indian traditions. Ashley's been trying to learn on her own and took up basket weaving only recently."

"What a smart thing for her to do," Abby said. "Learning about her roots will be good for her."

"I think so. She's a shy little thing and very pretty. I told her to come over for the festival and I'd introduce her to some of the other women in the tribe. A few may even remember her mother."

"That would be wonderful. I'm so glad

201

you met her and are taking her under your wing."

"Just like a mother hen, huh?" Wilma laughed and held out her arms wide, as though ready to embrace the world. "Just as well, I have plenty of wingspan."

"And a generous heart," Abby pointed out with a smile.

Pleased that Wilma had located the young woman, Abby went to her office and shrugged out of her windbreaker, hanging it on the back of the door. By exploring her ancestry and the customs of her mother's people, Ashley Tomlins had no doubt been trying to learn about herself and how she fit into the world. Not an easy thing for any adolescent to do, particularly on their own.

Wilma would make sure the girl felt that she was welcome and belonged among the Lummi, who were rightfully proud of their heritage.

The salesman of the nanny cams met Abby and Rick on Friday morning at Holloway's Hardware. A slender young man in his midtwenties with short blond hair, Gene Vandercamp exuded the high energy of an engine revved up on jet fuel and talked like a machine gun in overdrive.

"See, we've got just about any kind of

remote camera kit you could want. We got connectivity via LAN, modem, Bluetooth, infrared and anything else you can think of." He made a sweeping gesture that took in an array of electronic gadgets he'd spread out on the counter. "We got serial and parallel ports, wireless, quads and multiplexers. It's all vandal-proof and waterproof. Plus there's tech assistance at your fingertips twenty-four seven."

"Gene," Abby interrupted. "You need to slow down for us nontechnical folks. About the only thing I understood was that your equipment's waterproof."

"Oh, sorry, Dr. Stanton." His cheeks flushed. "I've always been a geek. Grew up on an Iowa farm, which wasn't exactly high tech. I couldn't afford to go to college, so I joined the Navy. Spent five years learning all kinds of electronic stuff and then when I got out, I got this job. I'm the sales rep for the whole Northwest, which is really cool."

"I'm sure it is," she said. "Now tell me slowly how the equipment will work if we put three cameras out in the field and want to monitor and record what's happening back here in town."

"That's easy, ma'am." He began again using less jargon and at a pace that allowed for questions.

As Abby tried to absorb the information, she noted Gene had the long fingers of an artist or a piano player. Dressed in a short-sleeved tan shirt and brown slacks, the pattern in his matching tie appeared to be miniature electronic circuit boards.

"We can link however many computers you want to the cameras via satellite or Wi-Fi, if the island's rigged for that."

"We're lucky to get our cell phones to work," Rick commented. Dressed casually like Abby, he had on jeans and a long-sleeved work shirt with the cuffs folded back.

Gene looked surprised. "Wow, you guys maybe need a new service provider. Somebody who can bring you into the twenty-first century."

"Hey, man," Aaron said, grinning. "We got folks out here who aren't all that comfortable with the twentieth century yet. Give us a break, huh?"

Amused, Abby could understand why Gene hadn't been happy in a quiet farming community.

"Why don't you suggest which three of these cameras will work best for us," she said.

He glanced between her and Rick, then over to Aaron. "You the one who's gonna install the gear?"

Aaron shook his head. "I gotta work, man. Abby and Rick will handle it."

Serious doubt flicked in Gene's eyes. "Tell you what, folks. Why don't I come along and show you how it's done. Then we'll know for sure if it's working. I want to be able to talk up the equipment around town, you know, for security uses — to spot stuff like pilfering, graffiti, vandalism. This will be the first job I've put together out here in the islands."

"We'd be happy to have your help, Gene," Abby said, more than a little relieved that she and Rick wouldn't have to master a complicated setup on their own.

"Great." He started to gather up his equipment. "We'll go in my van, if that's okay with you guys. I've got all my tools with me."

"We're going to need an extension ladder," Rick told him. "I've got one in my truck."

"No problem. We can lash it on top of the van."

Abby couldn't recall a more eager salesman or one more helpful. If he approached all of his potential customers with this much enthusiasm, she was confident he'd have a successful career.

The back of Gene's van did indeed look like an electronics lab, all tricked out with a worktable, test equipment and tiny drawers filled with component parts. Stacks of recording devices fit neatly into cubicles with bungee cords holding them in place.

"I really love this part of the country." Driving with ease, Gene maneuvered the van along Wayfarer Point Road toward the lighthouse. "Iowa's so flat with nothin' but cornfields for miles and miles, it's a real treat to see pine trees and firs plus a mountain or two now and then. I can hardly wait till I can get my family moved out here."

"You're married?" Abby asked, although she'd already noticed the gold band on his ring finger. She was sitting in the front passenger seat while Rick sat behind Gene.

"You bet. Three years now. I married my high school sweetheart while I was in the Navy. Couldn't stand being away from her. That's why I got out of the Navy." With one hand, he dug out his wallet from his back pocket and flipped it open to a snapshot of a blonde woman holding a tow-headed little boy. "My wife's Veronica. The boy's named Perry, after his great-grandfather. That's on my wife's side of the family. He turned two a month ago. Boy, I miss him too."

"I'm sure you do. He's adorable, and your wife's lovely." She held up the snapshot for Rick to see.

"Nice," Rick commented, meeting Abby's smile with one of his own.

"I'm thinking I'll be able to buy a small house outside of Bellingham. Nothing real big but maybe with some trees and a big yard for Perry to play in. I saved up some money while I was in the service. Not much to spend your dough on except sunscreen when you're floating around on a cruiser in the Mediterranean."

"I know whatever house you end up buying, you and your wife will turn it into a lovely home."

As the paved road ran out and turned to dirt, Gene slowed the van. Soon the lighthouse appeared and with it the sight of the straits beyond the point.

"Wow! Spectacular view. I bet it'd cost a pretty penny to build a house out here." He pulled to a stop and shifted into Park.

"It probably would, except the Coast Guard owns this land now. Which is nice, because that way we can all enjoy the view."

They climbed out of the van, and the two men untied the ladder from the roof of the vehicle. They all trudged to the base of the lighthouse. Rick showed Gene where he thought the camera should be mounted.

"Tell me again why we're doing this?" he asked, scrambling up the ladder to take a closer look.

Briefly, Rick told him how counterfeiters were providing forged IDs and using geo-cache sites for their illegal scheme.

Gene dropped down to the ground look-ing determined, his jaw tight and his brows lowered. "I'll get you some nice clear shots so you can ID the guy."

It took Gene, with Rick's help, an hour to mount the camera and make sure he could receive the image on his computer, which was in the van.

"I'll give you the Internet address I've set up and the password when we're done here. You'll be able to access the pictures in real time or record them, whichever you want."

"Will we be able to see all three camera locations at once?" Abby asked.

"You bet. I'll fix you up with a split screen."

"How about hackers?" Rick wanted to know. "How secure is your setup?"

"The most secure available. I've tried to hack into the system myself. It took me a week, and I know how the firewall operates."

Feeling confident the first installation was working as intended, they drove back into town, had lunch at the Springhouse Café, then went to Paradise Cove.

When Gene had the camera in place under the eaves of the Lynches' boathouse, he showed them how the split screen worked.

"See?" He pointed to the picture of a couple strolling across the rocky point hand-in-hand not far from the lighthouse. "You can zoom in or get a wide shot."

At the corner of the picture when he widened out the shot, Abby could see the fender of a car, although she couldn't identify the model. About then, the couple turned to each other and began to kiss.

"I'm feeling a bit like a voyeur," she said.

"Nowadays, there are so many cameras around — at intersections and train stations, everywhere — nobody can be sure of their privacy anymore," Rick commented.

Abby wasn't a hundred percent sure that was a good thing. She supposed it was simply a sign of the times.

They went out to Oyster Inlet, where Gene had to climb a tree to gain a suitable vantage point without risking that the equipment would be spotted and possibly stolen. Then they returned to the Nature Museum to hook up the recorder and make sure Abby could bring up the surveillance video on her computer.

At the end of the day, when she and Rick watched the ferry pull away from the dock with Gene and his portable electronics lab onboard, Abby sighed.

"Now all we have to do is wait," she said.

A few minutes later, as she was on her way home, she had a call on her cell phone from Henry Cobb. She pulled over so she could talk.

"I got a report back from Agent Burns," he said. "He had someone trace the suspect messages on your geocaching Web site back to the Internet service providers and then to the specific computers they came from."

"Terrific. What'd he find out?"

"Not particularly good news. All of the messages came from computers used by the public at libraries."

Her heart sank with disappointment. Adjusting her glasses, she pressed her thumb and finger to the bridge of her nose. "So there's no way to know who actually sent the messages."

"He's got people talking to the librarians.

They may have a record of who was using the computer at the time the messages were sent."

"Then there's still hope of tracing the individual?"

"Some, but I'm not optimistic. Chances are good they didn't use their real names."

In the background, Abby heard one of his deputies talking to Henry. It was a moment before he returned to her.

"The reasonably good news is that the message sent to HeeHaw about his cache being muggled originated at the Sparrow Island Library," Henry said. "I'm going over there now to talk to Naomi. See if she can help us out. I thought you might like to be there."

"Absolutely."

Excited about possibly gleaning some good news, as soon as the road was clear, Abby made a U-turn and headed back into town. Naomi Yardley was the head librarian as well as the de facto historian of Sparrow Island. There was little she didn't know about the community, and she could pluck the title of a book or its author from thin air with only the slightest hint about the subject.

Located on Kingfisher Street, not far from Green Harbor Public School, the library

211

was small but carried a surprising array of titles.

Abby hurried to the entrance. It was almost closing time and the library was quiet, the last few patrons checking out their books.

Henry was already there talking with Naomi. They both acknowledged Abby's arrival with a nod.

"As I was telling Henry," Naomi said, "I recall seeing the man he's interested in, the one in the photograph, but I don't recall much about him. He seemed perfectly normal to me. Remember, we have three computers for the public to use. I don't keep track of everyone who drops by."

"He wasn't angry?" Abby asked. His e-mail had certainly been testy.

Naomi considered her question, fiddling with the glasses that hung around her neck on a silver chain. "No, I don't think so. It's been a week. I simply don't recall anything about him that stood out."

Henry asked, "Do you have records of who was on a computer at a particular time?"

"Yes, of course." Not a very tall woman and rather slender, she hurried behind the main checkout counter. She drew out a long drawer that apparently contained the records of who had been using the computers and when. She sorted through the four-by-six cards, then lifted her head. "I think this is the one." She passed the card over to Henry.

"John Smith," he read, doubt lacing his voice.

"That's what he put down." Stretching herself across the counter, she looked at the card she'd given Henry. "I'm sure the clerk must have asked him for an ID."

"Or not," he mumbled.

"I'm sorry, Sergeant. I guess I should tighten up on our procedures."

"It's okay, Naomi." Henry handed her back the card. "You had no idea we'd be trying to track down this man, or anybody else who uses your computers."

"It's mostly kids," she said. "Not every family can afford a computer. Sometimes their homework demands that they log onto the Internet to do research. We want to do what we can to help them. Of course, we always block out Web sites that might be too mature for the youngsters."

"We understand," Abby told her.

As Abby and Henry left the library, Abby said, "So our presumed illegal alien was here, and was also at the café according to Ida, and he sent a message to his contact via HeeHaw's posting. So who was he really trying to communicate with? HeeHaw? Or his contact in the counterfeit ring?"

Henry stopped on the sidewalk, glanced up and down the street and shook his head. "I have no idea."

CHAPTER THIRTEEN

On Sunday, Abby woke to a pewter sky and drizzling rain.

Drops formed on the eaves outside her bedroom window as she read her morning devotions. Slowly they released their grip on the edge of the roof, plunging to the ground to nurture the flowers below. Trees that had grown dusty in the recent dry spell put on their brightest green coats. Newly washed, the weathered cedar fence in the backyard glistened as though nature had applied a fresh coat of paint.

Finished with the reading, Abby bowed her head and prayed. "Lord, help me to meet this day with the same fresh spirit You bring to all that is here on earth. Let me remember You in all that I do and give thanks for Your presence. Amen."

Standing, she stretched and went to her desk, where she booted up her laptop computer. Yesterday she'd gone by the museum to check the tape for activity at the cache sites. There'd been little at any of the three, and no indication that anyone had planted forged documents. Or was even geocaching just for fun.

Now when she brought up the split screen in real time, she got gray misty pictures of the three locations. No early walkers appeared in the scene at Wayfarer Point; the Lynches' dock stood vacant in the rain, and there were no hikers passing near the cache at Oyster Inlet. Although she could make out the familiar landmarks in each setting, the light rain obscured the details of the stage she, Rick and Gene had set to catch a crook.

"Apparently criminals are finding other things to do with their time on a rainy Sunday," she said out loud.

Logging off her computer, she showered and dressed in a skirt and blouse, then went downstairs for breakfast. She found Mary in the kitchen.

"Yum. Something smells delicious," Abby said.

"I was up early and thought I'd make some banana nut muffins for our breakfast, then take some to Mom and Dad for Sunday supper." The stove timer dinged, and she wheeled over to remove the tin with a dozen plump muffins baked toasty brown. "You're just in time to give them the taste test."

"I'm confident they'll pass with flying colors." Although Abby could find her way around a kitchen when she needed to, there was no question that her sister was the better cook. And that was just fine with Abby. She got the benefit of delicious homemade meals without having to do the work. "Dad will be pleased about the muffins. They're one of his favorites."

"That's because I use Mom's recipe."

Abby got glasses down from the cupboard and poured orange juice for them both, then fixed herself a cup of coffee. She sat down at the kitchen table where the place mats Mary had set out were decorated with colorful appliquéd tulips on a lavender background.

Blossom, her tail standing up straight, trotted into the kitchen, apparently deciding to have her breakfast too.

Delivering the muffins to the table, Mary said, "Be careful. These will be hot. I don't want you to burn your tongue."

"Yes, Mother," Abby teased, chuckling. "So how are the plans going for the festival?"

"Everything seems to be in order. There'll

be a big article in the *Birdcall* in Wednesday's edition, and Keith Gordon's made posters to put in storefronts. The town's putting up banners on the light poles, as well. My big worry now is that it not rain next weekend."

Using her fork, Abby broke open the muffin and watched the steam rise along with the warm scent of freshly baked bread. "The last weather report I saw predicted this will be a short storm, gone by tomorrow, and then we'll have clear skies the rest of the week."

"I hope they're right. June weather can be unpredictable." She bowed her head in prayer for a moment before starting on her muffin. "I gather your hidden cameras haven't detected any miscreants so far or you would have said something."

"All's quiet at the moment. I do plan to go by the museum after we have supper with the folks and check the tape. If whoever's planting the fake documents is smart, he may wait till it's sunny."

"Maybe he'll think the rain is a good cover."

Abby supposed that was possible. The weather would certainly keep most people away from the cache sites, making it less likely the criminal would be spotted and identified later.

When they finished breakfast, they cleaned up the kitchen and got ready for church. Because of Abby's plan to check the video tapes later at the museum, they went in separate vehicles.

Abby and Mary arrived just as their parents settled into their usual pew. The rain hadn't deterred many members of the congregation, and Rev. Hale had a nearly full house for his sermon. Using Psalms 95 as his Scripture reading, the pastor spoke of the many ways people can worship the Lord: here in church through the rituals and symbols portrayed within God's house, out in nature where the hand of God is apparent, and in caring for those in need. Love for God can be expressed through either meditation or song, or both, he reminded them.

By the time the service was over, Mary felt renewed and ready to worship the Lord in every way she could as the week progressed.

The congregation began to file out of the church. As she moved with the crowd, greeting her friends, Mary noticed Bobby trudging along the walkway wearing only a light jacket as protection against the misting rain.

"Hey, Bobby, I'll share my umbrella, if

you'd like," she offered.

His weary sigh was enough to blow out the candles on a hundred-year-old's birthday cake. "Okay."

She tugged him up close to her and held the umbrella so he'd stay dry. "What's wrong?"

"Mom says Dad and I can't go fishing 'cuz it's raining."

"That's too bad, but she's probably worried you'll catch a cold."

He looked at her with eyes so forlorn, it seemed the world must soon be coming to an end. "Yeah, I know. But we've only caught one good bass so far, a two-and-a-half-pounder. That's not big enough to win the Bass Classic."

"There's still a week left until the festival, and it's supposed to be good weather all week."

"But Dad's gotta work. We won't be able to go fishing again till next Saturday. That's the very last day of the contest."

She ran a soothing hand over his damp, brown hair. "I'll just bet you that the fish will be extra hungry by then and ready to jump right on your hook."

His narrow shoulders slumped. "I sure hope so. I heard there's a *girl* who's winning so far."

She nearly choked on a laugh. "Well, you know Abby and I will be rooting for you, Bobby. Of course, if the girl wins, we know you'll be a good sport about it."

His scowl told Mary he'd have to work at his good sportsmanship skills if the worst happened.

His mother called him then, and Bobby went running off, unconcerned by a bit of rain. Mary remembered Zack had hated to wear a raincoat unless it was pouring buckets. "None of the guys do," he'd insisted. She'd been lucky to get him to wear a baseball cap and a regular jacket on rainy days.

She heard her name spoken and turned to find Ileana Zeklos and young Caterina walking up behind her.

"Good morning, Mary," Ileana said in her softly accented voice. "How are you today?"

"I'm quite well, thank you. Hello, Caterina. What a pretty dress you're wearing."

Standing very close to her mother, Caterina smiled shyly. "My mother make it."

"She did a good job." To a jumper pattern, Ileana had added short sleeves in a fabric printed with delicate roses that matched the rosy color of the dress itself.

"Caterina made something at Vacation Bible School for you and your sister." Ileana urged her daughter forward.

In the child's hand, she held a folded piece of what looked to be a sheet of drawing paper. She held it out for Mary to take.

"Why, thank you, Caterina." Mary glanced around to find Abby, and beckoned her over. "Let's see what Caterina has made for us."

As Mary opened the paper, Abby leaned over her shoulder.

"It's a picture of Comoară," Abby exclaimed.

"What a pretty kitty," Mary said, noticing the detail of the cat's white paws. "I particularly like the halo you put around Comoară's head. Did you make this all by yourself?"

"I drawed it in school," the child said, her expression full of shy pride. "Como is a good kitty. I love her."

"It's beautiful," Abby said.

Mary's chest tightened around a different kind of love, a love for this sweet little girl. "I bet I can find a magnet at home and we'll put your picture up on our refrigerator so we can see it every day. Would that be all right with you?"

Ileana spoke to her daughter in Romanian, and then said, "You are both so kind. We wish we had more ways to thank you. Yousef wishes that, too, but he is at work today."

"This is more than enough," Mary said. "The picture is precious to us, just like Co-moară is to you."

When Caterina giggled, Mary suspected she'd mispronounced the unfamiliar word and laughed along with the girl. But in the child's happy laughter, she recognized the joy she felt was yet another way to worship the Lord and give thanks for His blessings.

Abby knew she'd indulged in too much of her mother's fresh peach cobbler at supper. She roughly estimated that she'd need to hike to the top of Arrowhead Mountain sixteen times to use up the calories she'd consumed.

But every bite was worth it, she thought as she walked into her office at the Nature Museum and shed her raincoat. Rain had fallen steadily all day and it was still misting outside. Only dull gray light filtered in through the window, and she switched on her desk light to compensate.

Checking the computer, she discovered at least one camera's motion detector had been activated. Anticipation stirred in her midsection as she loaded the video and sat down in front of her computer to see who or what had been near the caches.

The first scene appeared. According to the time stamp at the bottom of the screen, Wayfarer Point had played host to a large crow who'd grown curious about the camera lens early this morning. He pecked at the unfamiliar object. His yellow eyes looked huge on the screen, his beak a deadly weapon.

"Get away from there!" Abby ordered, to no avail.

He pecked at the object again, and Abby cringed. She hoped the silly bird wouldn't damage the expensive equipment. Gene Vandercamp would have trouble explaining the loss to his boss.

Having failed to dislodge the camera, and finding it worthless as food, the crow flew off toward the tree line.

A moment later the screen flickered. The Lynches' dock came into focus. A small boat with an outboard motor eased up to the end of the dock from the right of the screen; a single individual wearing a hooded rain jacket steered from the back. *A man,* Abby thought.

He idled the engine and grabbed onto the dock to hold the boat in place, then looked around the cove as though making sure no one was observing him.

Abby leaned forward as the man ducked

his head out of sight below the dock.

"No! Stay where I can see you."

He had to be checking the cache Rick had discovered under the dock. But Abby couldn't see if he was placing something there or removing the cache.

"Lift your head. Please." She willed him to give her a good look at his face. But when his head appeared again, the hood on his rain jacket hid all but a quick shot of his profile when he glanced around furtively again.

The time stamp read 13:32. The man had been at the dock at one thirty that afternoon. It was after three o'clock now. He'd be gone by this time.

On the screen, he didn't look like a big man. Not a boy either. But it was hard to tell anything about his size or age as he swung the boat out into the cove and turned it toward the open sea, motoring out of range of the camera.

Frantic to get a better look at the stranger, she started the clip over and watched it in slow motion. That didn't help much. So she ran it again and again. Between the hood and the misting rain, she couldn't identify the man. His features were either hidden or blurred.

The best she could tell, based on the quick

flash of his profile and the complexion of his bare hands, the man could be an African American. But she couldn't even be sure of that.

Leaning back in her chair, she removed her glasses and rubbed her eyes. She'd call Henry Cobb, let him take a look at the video.

Henry arrived at the museum in less than fifteen minutes. He took off his hat and sat down in the chair Abby relinquished to him. "Let's see what you've got."

"I'm not sure. Maybe the guy who's stashing the phony IDs. Or maybe just a regular geocacher out for an afternoon hunt."

"In the rain in an open boat?" Henry added with a doubtful shake of his head.

She keyed up the footage and ran it for him, then repeated the same scene in slow motion.

"There! What's that on the side of the boat?" Henry pointed to the screen just as the boat reached the dock on the third viewing. "Back it up a few frames."

She did as he asked, then ran the video forward again.

"Stop right there." Squinting, Henry stared at the screen. "The guy is hard to make out, but see those markings on the side of the boat."

"Yes. A name?"

"More than that." He leaned back with a satisfied smile. "It's the Dorset's logo. That's one of their rental boats."

Abby looked again. "You're absolutely right! And if someone rented the boat, they'll have a record of who it was."

"Let's hope so. But first we have to see if he actually planted anything illegal at that cache site and retrieve the evidence if he did." Picking up his hat, he stood. "Let's make a DVD of the footage and bring it along. Maybe Keith Gordon or one of his staff will be able to recognize our man."

Abby burned the DVD and took one more look at the live shots of the cache sites before turning off her computer. In the rainy gloom, no one was within camera range.

Pulling on her raincoat, she dropped the DVD in her pocket and followed Henry out the door to his patrol car. Her heart was beating fast and adrenaline flooded her veins. Now they had a good shot at identifying at least one culprit involved in the forgery ring.

Henry drove directly to Paradise Cove and parked at the foot of the Lynches' dock.

"You can wait in the car, if you want," he

said to Abby. "No need for you to get wet too."

"I'll have to show you where the cache is."

She got out of the car, and together they walked to the end of the dock. The scene looked much as it had on the video, except there was no boat there. She started to kneel down.

"Let me do that," Henry said. "You'll ruin your skirt."

Of course, he'd likely get the knees of his dark green uniform pants dirty, but Abby didn't point that out. She'd let him be the gentleman. "The cache should be right under this middle board. If the man we saw planted something else, it'll be behind the cache box, probably on a crosspiece, like Rick said."

Getting down on his knees, Henry leaned over the edge of the dock. "I see it." A moment later, he held up the Styrofoam box Rick had found when they first discovered the cache site.

"Look on a crossbeam behind where the box was. See if there's anything that looks out of place."

Setting the box aside, he bent over again. "Yep. We've got the same kind of tubular container as the other one you brought me, and it's taped to a strut with duct tape."

He took a moment to put on latex gloves that he'd had in his pocket and bent to the task again.

Abby waited expectantly until he finally sat back on his haunches, a metal tube in his hand.

"We've got him now," Abby said.

"Not exactly. Assuming there are forged documents in here, we have some evidence of a crime. But we don't have the perpetrator. Yet." He came to his feet with ease. "And when we do identify the guy on the video, let's hope he can lead us to the counterfeiting ring."

Back in the car, Henry carefully opened the container and used tweezers to lift the documents out one by one. Two green cards and driver's licenses this time, one each for Andrea and Pablo Rodriguez from Mexico. Or so the IDs claimed.

"It must have cost a bundle to buy these," Henry commented as he slid the counterfeits back into the container and then put the tube in an evidence bag, taping it shut. "Let's get over to the Dorset and see what we can find out there."

At the Dorset's private dock, a half-dozen small boats like the one on the video bobbed forlornly, tethered to mooring cleats, their outboard motors apparently stowed in the boathouse. The same number of rental kayaks were stacked along the length of the wooden dock, and Keith Gordon's classic cabin cruiser was moored at the end slip. No one was around to rent a boat to a hotel guest, had there been anyone interested.

"Not exactly a busy day for boaters," Henry commented.

"Maybe someone at the front desk will be able to help us."

Making a U-turn, Henry drove back to the circular drive near the hotel entrance and parked in front of the stone fountain. The drizzling rain mixed with the spraying water from the fountain, and pooled around the sculpture.

The doorman opened the large brass door to the hotel for them. "Good afternoon, Dr. Stanton. Sergeant. I hope there's no problem here."

"Nothing to worry about, Muldoon," Henry assured the doorman. "We just need to speak to someone at the front desk for a moment."

Muldoon nodded slightly, gesturing toward the registration desk. "Of course. I'm sure they'll be happy to assist you."

There was only one clerk behind the cherrywood registration counter, a young man so slender his jacket hung from his shoulders with as much style as it would on a coat hanger. Cameron welcomed them with a cheerful smile.

"Good afternoon. How may I help you folks today?"

Henry got right to the point. "We'd like to know who rented any of the Dorset's boats today."

"We went by the dock, but there was no one there," Abby added.

Cameron looked surprised. "I don't believe we rent boats when it's raining, sir. Staff assigned to that service would be reassigned to other activities or given the day off."

"Can you make sure of that?" Henry asked.

"Yes, sir. I'll check with Mr. Gordon, if you'd like."

Henry nodded, indicating that's exactly what he'd like.

Turning away from the reception counter, Abby surveyed the opulent lobby. Only a few chairs were occupied, the guests conversing in near whispers. Lamps on end tables cast soft light. The gray day gave the room a sleepy feeling, and she yawned in spite of herself.

"Been staying up late these days?" Henry teased.

She chuckled. "Not really. This kind of weather always does me in."

He nodded and turned just as Keith Gordon approached.

The owner of the Dorset extended his hand to Abby. "Good to see you, my dear. And you, Sergeant." He shook hands with Henry as well. Impeccably dressed, he wore a grey suit with a light-blue silk tie. "Cameron tells me you have a question about our rental boats."

"That's right. Did any of your boats go out today?" Henry asked.

"Specifically, were any of them out around one thirty this afternoon?" Abby clarified.

"Not that I'm aware of. If someone had wanted to rent a boat, which would be a bit unusual on a day like this, he would have asked at the front desk. No one has, to my knowledge."

"Interesting." Holding his hat in his hand, Henry ran his fingers around the brim. "Do you have a computer nearby? I'd like you to take a look at something."

Curious, Keith arched his brows. "Of course. In my office. Please follow me."

He led them down a quiet corridor. On a Sunday afternoon, most of the offices were empty, the desks cleared of papers. Soft mood music played through invisible speakers.

At the end of the hallway, they entered Keith's office, the carpet a bit thicker than in the corridor, the mahogany desk and credenza larger and more elegant than the furniture in the offices of his staff members. A large window provided a view of the inner courtyard. The walls were painted hunter green with a dark wood wainscoting covering the lower few feet.

Keith touched a button, and a portion of one wall slid open to reveal an entertainment center with a large TV screen, DVD player and VCR.

Abby handed him the DVD.

"Can you tell me what this is all about?" he asked as he slipped it into the machine.

"Let's first see if you can identify the person on the video," Henry said. Using the remote, he started the DVD.

Stroking his white goatee thoughtfully, Keith watched the footage. When the segment ended, he said, "It's hard to make out the details in the rain. Where was this taken?"

"Paradise Cove," Abby said. "Earlier this afternoon."

"First, is that one of your boats?" Henry

asked as he played the DVD again.

"Yes. Yes, it looks like one of ours. What's that man doing?"

"Do you recognize him?" Henry persisted.

"He looks familiar. So does his rain jacket. We issue those to all of our new staff members along with their appropriate uniforms." Frowning, his white eyebrows lowering in concentration, Keith gestured for Henry to play the video one more time. "I can't be one hundred percent sure, but the man could be one of our housekeeping staff. A young man from Belize named Damani."

CHAPTER FOURTEEN

Keith sent a bellman to locate Damani and asked him to come to the office. While they waited, Henry explained the situation to Keith and their suspicions regarding Damani's involvement in the counterfeit ring.

Keith shook his head. "I'm truly surprised Damani would be involved in any criminal activity. He's been an outstanding employee since he arrived. I know he's been hoping he'd be invited to return next year and someday immigrate permanently."

"Maybe he found a way to speed up the process by skipping a few steps," Henry commented.

"If he's guilty, his dreams will be lost," Keith said. "I don't know how he or anyone else could risk such dire consequences. I know I never would have."

Abby's excitement about identifying a criminal had given way to concern that a young man might well have ruined his life and his future. It was one thing to lock up a counterfeiter who was knowingly preying on those who longed for a better life in the States. It was quite another matter to destroy the life of a young man who simply delivered a package to a location as directed by a higher-up in an illegal scheme.

After a soft knock on Keith's office door, Damani entered. He was dressed in jeans and sandals along with a white dress shirt that looked as though he'd hastily tucked in the tail.

"You wanted to see me, sir?" he asked Keith politely, giving Henry a quick glance in the process.

Keith made the introductions. "Sergeant Cobb wants to ask you a few questions."

Looking wary, Damani said, "Yes, sir?"

"Where were you earlier this afternoon?" Henry asked.

"I have been in my room most of the day, sir. Some of us were going to town, but decided not to because of the rain."

"Our summer staff lives in dorm rooms in a separate building on the property," Keith explained.

They'd all remained standing, Keith behind his desk, Abby and Henry near the television screen and DVD player.

"Did you borrow one of the hotel's boats

236

this afternoon?" Henry asked.

"Oh no, sir. Not today. Sometimes a mate and I will take out a boat on our days off if no guest wants them. But not today." His dark eyes were wide with worry. "Am I in trouble, sir?"

"Guess you'll have to tell us." Henry played the DVD. "Is that you in the boat?"

Almost as tall as Henry, the young man leaned forward. "Oh no, sir." He exhaled audibly as though the weight of the world had been lifted from his shoulders. "That is not me."

"Do you know who it is?" Abby asked.

He glanced toward her. "If I tell you, will he be in trouble?"

"If you *don't* tell us," Henry emphasized, "I guarantee you'll be the one in trouble."

Damani grimaced. "That is Remijio Bejos. We call him Remi. He is one of us from Belize."

"Are you sure?" Abby questioned.

Keith sat down at his desk and booted up his computer, his fingers moving quickly over the keyboard.

"Yes, ma'am. I do not want to get him in trouble. He is my countryman. But he is the one in the video, not me. Has he done something wrong?"

Looking up from his computer, Keith

said, "Bejos is assigned to our gardening staff. He's been here about six weeks. His supervisor has issued a couple of warnings about his work habits, but no serious reprimands."

"Let's get him down here so we can talk to him too," Henry said. "Damani can stay in one of the other offices while we figure out what's going on."

Keith opened the door to an adjacent conference room, indicating Damani could wait there.

Looking worried, Damani hesitated at the doorway and spoke to Henry. "Please, sir, Remi has many brothers and sisters at home. His mother is sick and cannot work. I do not know what he has done, but I do know his family has sent him here to make money for them. His life has not been easy."

"I'll keep that in mind, son," Henry said.

Placing a call to the bell captain, Keith asked him to have someone track Remi down.

The wait was longer this time. Suspecting she wouldn't be getting home anytime soon, Abby called Mary to let her know she was with Henry and briefly told her about the situation.

When Remijio finally appeared, he looked both scared and rebellious, his jaw tight, his dark eyes flashing. His complexion as dark as Damani's, Remi was shorter and stockier than his countryman and his arms more heavily muscled, as though he was used to hard labor.

Henry began his questioning in the same way he had with Damani. At first Remi denied having taken a boat to Paradise Cove. Then, shown the video, he admitted he had been there but insisted that he'd done nothing wrong. He'd been bored and had gone for a boat ride, that was all.

"Young man, you're involved in a ring of counterfeiters," Henry told him, his voice stern. "That's a serious federal offense in this country. If you don't tell me exactly what's going on, I'll be forced to turn you over to federal authorities. They'll lock you up and you won't see Belize and your home or family again for a very long time."

Stalling, the young man managed to lift his chin belligerently. "I am in this country legally. I have rights."

"You bet you do, son." Henry produced a pair of handcuffs. "You have the right to remain silent. What you say can and will be used against you. If you need an attorney and cannot —"

"All right! I'll tell you what you want to know. But I don't want to go to jail, okay?"

Now he appeared shaken and on the verge of tears.

"We'll talk about that *after* you tell me everything I want to know," Henry promised.

It was after dark before Henry had finished his interrogation of Remi, and Abby finally was able to drive home.

"Gracious, I've been worried about you." Sitting in her favorite chair in the living room, Mary set her knitting aside when Abby came in. "I'm so glad you called to warn me you'd be late or I would have been out searching for you myself."

Finnegan stood and stretched, wagging his tail in greeting. Blossom, curled up in another chair, opened one eye, then blinked it closed.

"Turned out to be a long afternoon." Collapsing onto the couch, Abby leaned back and closed her eyes. "But we caught the young man who's been planting the fake documents at the cache sites. He's from Belize."

"Oh no! I hope it wasn't Damani at the Dorset. He seemed like such a nice young man."

Removing her glasses, Abby rubbed her eyes. "At first we thought Damani was the one we were after. Fortunately for him, he was able to identify one of his compatriots on the video we had, a young man who was hired on the gardening crew. His name's Remi Bejos."

Mary nodded knowingly. "I remember seeing a couple of young fellows working in the gardens. I had no idea . . ."

"Keith Gordon didn't either and wasn't in the least pleased to find out one of his people was involved in the scheme."

"How on earth did this Remi get hooked into a counterfeiting ring?"

"Apparently, after he was offered a job at the Dorset via an employment agency that was recruiting in Belize, another man contacted him. They promised him two hundred dollars for each job he did for them. He had no idea he was dealing with an illegal immigration scam."

Finnegan strolled over to Abby and rested his head on her knee, asking for a pet, which she willingly provided along with a few scratches behind his ears.

"This stranger," Abby continued, "showed Remi how to use the geocaching Web site and even gave him a GPS unit to use."

"That's an expensive gadget to give away."

"Probably an incidental expense to these guys. Hardly worth counting when you think of the money they must be charging the immigrants for such high-tech counterfeits, documents that are very hard to detect.

"Anyway, after Remi arrived at the Dorset, he sent an e-mail message to either the stranger he'd met or someone else. He's not sure. And he gave him his mailing address. Four times since he arrived in early May when spring landscaping gets underway, he's received a package in the mail that contained a metal tube like Rick and I found at Oyster Inlet."

Abby was still amazed how complicated the scheme had been, and how well it had worked until she and Rick had stumbled on the first cache site.

"Remi was just a small cog in a much larger international scheme. His job was to hide the tube at a cache site, then use the Sparrow Island Library computers to let his boss know where he'd planted the documents. He'd been told to use caches that were accessible by boat, although he wasn't told why. But that meant he'd have to borrow one of the Dorset's rental boats at a time when hotel guests weren't likely to want them.

"Using the library computer, he e-mailed his contact that he'd placed the package at a cache site. That person apparently had a method of contacting the buyer of the documents to let him know where he would find them, using the code number of the cache site. About a week after Remi did his job, assuming the documents had been successfully delivered, Remi would get another package. Two hundred dollars in cash. Apparently his employer was extremely upset when the documents Rick and I found didn't get delivered to the customer. Remi had to beg the man to keep him on the payroll. It's that person, the ringleader of the outfit, that Henry and I want to see caught and held accountable."

Shaking her head, Mary said, "Dear me, whoever would have thought computers meant to be used by the public for good would be used for such a scheme?"

"It certainly makes it hard to trace anyone who's involved."

Looking out the sliding glass door, Abby could see a bit of moonlight on the trees beyond the back fence. The sky had begun to clear and they'd have fair weather tomorrow.

"Will Henry be able to track down the ringleader now?" Mary asked.

"He thinks Agent Burns of Immigration and Customs Enforcement will be able to, now that we have an e-mail address and the name of the Internet service provider. Meanwhile, we'll keep trying to pick up new leads here to uncover the instigators of the scheme."

"What about the young man, Remi? What will become of him?"

"Henry thinks, because Remi cooperated, that he'll avoid jail time, although the young man is currently a guest in one of Henry's cells. Eventually, Remi will probably be deported."

"I understand why, but it's sad, isn't it?" Mary said.

"More than you know. Remi's mother has been ill and isn't able to work. He's sent almost every bit of money he's earned this summer — including what he made illegally — home to Belize."

"His family situation is what made him an easy target for the man who recruited him initially. I imagine two hundred dollars would go a long way in Belize."

"You're absolutely right," Abby agreed. "With any luck, the Belize authorities will be able to find that man, Remi's initial contact, and bring him to justice."

Mary picked up her knitting again. "I believe I'll include the young man in my prayers tonight. It sounds like Remi could use a little extra help from the Lord to see him through this difficult time."

Abby agreed with her sister's sentiment and vowed to add Remi to her prayers as well.

Early Monday morning, Abby got a call from Henry. He wanted her to meet him at the library when it opened at ten o'clock. Agent Burns had asked them to set a trap for the person who planned to pick up the forged documents that had been planted at Paradise Cove.

Abby and Henry arrived at the library just as Naomi Yardley unlocked the front doors.

Naomi greeted them with a pleasant smile. "You two are becoming regular library patrons, aren't you?"

Holding the door open for Abby, Henry said, "You have, by far, the best library on the island. We wouldn't think of going anywhere else."

Naomi chuckled since this was the only library on the island. "Is there something special I can do for you this morning? Or something I can help you find?"

"We'd like to use your computers, if that's all right," Abby said.

"Of course." With a worried frown, she glanced from Abby to Henry. "Did both of your hard discs crash at the same time?"

"Fortunately, no. But we do need to use a public computer today," Henry said.

"Ah, you're working on a case," she said.

"That's a safe assumption." Henry chose the third computer located along the far wall near the periodicals. He let Abby have the chair while he dragged up a second one. "Remi gave me the screen name he's been using and the e-mail address he sends messages to." He showed Abby a piece of paper with the information written on it as well as the format Remi used for his messages.

"So I'm going to pretend to be Remi?" she asked.

"Right. We're going to let our unknown counterfeiter believe the documents have been safely planted. Presumably he'll let the customer know, and they'll show up at Paradise Cove."

"Where we'll be waiting for them." Abby turned on the computer.

"I'll have my men stake out the cove during daylight hours. I don't have enough staff to watch the place around the clock, but I'll assume the subjects will show up during the day."

"That sounds reasonable to me. It wouldn't be smart to take a boat into an unfamiliar area in the dark."

"So that means we'll catch whoever shows

up on nanny cam. That should hold up in court."

Using her own screen name and password, Abby first went to the geocaching site to get the code number for the cache site in question. Then she signed off and signed on again using Remi's identification. Copying Remi's format, she wrote an e-mail to the address Remi had provided.

"This look right to you?" she asked.

"Yep. Let's send it."

With a click of the computer mouse, the message went out into cyber space, hopefully to the ringleader of the counterfeit gang.

"Agent Burns is tracking down the user of that e-mail address via the Internet service provider. Shouldn't take more than a day or two."

"It sounds like the feds have speeded things up, huh?"

"Right. Now that they know more about what's happening and the process, Burns is guessing there are more illegals coming into the States at other locations where they're using different package delivery people like Remi. You and Rick might have stumbled onto just one tentacle of a very large illegal enterprise."

It was a frightening thought to imagine

the number of people who were entering the country illegally as a result of this scheme. Abby realized the reasons those people were coming could be even more terrifying.

"Did Remi indicate whether he got a message back after he sent his e-mail?"

"Just the time you hijacked the delivery. Instead of a payoff, he got a nasty phone call."

"Any way to trace the call?"

Henry picked up the paper with the e-mail information, folding it in half again. "Agent Burns is working on that too. Frankly, I'd be surprised if the call's traceable. More than likely it came from a throwaway phone with a prepaid card."

"What we need is another lead. Someone who has access to the inner circle of the counterfeit ring."

"That's why we're setting this trap." He tapped the computer screen with his knuckle. "We're hoping the Rodriguez couple — if that's their real name — will be our link to the top dog."

"I wonder how long it will take them to show up."

"I showed the IDs to my men. No one remembers seeing the couple around here, so we don't think they're on Sparrow Island now. That means they're at least two hours away, if they're coming by boat."

"And Remi was instructed to use caches that were accessible by boat," she recalled. "So the couple could get here by ferry from Bellingham or Port Angeles, and then rent a boat."

"Or they could enter from Canada on a private boat and pick up their package that way."

With so many questions still unanswered, there was little Abby could do except make sure she had a new tape in the recorder and ready to go at the museum.

Uncovering Remi's involvement had produced only one piece of the puzzle. Uncovering the whole picture would require a good deal more information. And a lot of luck.

Abby spent the rest of the day in her office getting caught up on correspondence. She'd had a letter from a friend at Cornell. A gifted graduate student was hoping to find an internship on the West Coast and Abby's friend wanted to know if she knew of any opportunities.

Unfortunately, internships were few and far between in the field of ornithology. There was plenty of research that could be done, but funding was always a problem.

As Abby worked her way through her correspondence, she kept checking the live camera shot at Paradise Cove.

Switching from the screen to the live shot for the third time in the past hour, she spotted a couple of kids rowing a boat. The fact that they kept rowing in circles, unable to keep the boat going in a straight line, appeared to be hysterical. Their silent laughter made Abby wish she could join in the fun, and she recalled years ago a time she and her sister got into the same kind of giggly fit when they'd tried to synchronize their oars.

She smiled at the memory. It was a wonder they'd ever made it back to shore.

"Whatever you're thinking about must make you happy."

Abby started at Hugo's voice, and looked up. "You're right. I was just thinking about the good ol' days of summer fun like these youngsters are enjoying." She nodded toward her computer screen.

He stepped around so he could see what she was looking at. "Is this a movie?"

"No, it's a live shot of Paradise Cove." Briefly, she brought him up to date about the illegal immigrant scheme and what they'd learned so far.

"So you caught one of the parties to the

crime," he said when she finished.

"But not a key player. Henry and the federal agent are hopeful we can get one step closer to the top if we catch someone picking up the fake documents."

His hands linked behind his back, Hugo continued to watch the young people on the screen futilely attempting to get their little boat under control. Today he was dressed in a summer-weight navy blazer with tan slacks and cravat, a resort-elegant outfit suitable for a stay at the Dorset or a five star facility in Palm Springs, California.

"It seems unlikely your suspects will make their appearance while those youngsters are playing so close to the cache site," he said.

"True. But I can't seem to stop myself from taking a peek every now and then. We don't really know how long it's likely to be before someone shows up to claim their counterfeit treasure."

Deciding she'd seen enough for this afternoon, she switched the screen back to the letter she'd been writing.

"I think I'll finish up my sparrow survey tomorrow morning at the northwest corner of the island. There's some likely habitat not far from the shoreline. That will give me four different sample sites to use for baseline data. Resurveying the same areas every two to three years ought to give us a reasonable picture of the sparrow population and whether it's declining, as we suspect."

"An excellent plan. I'll look forward to reviewing your initial data."

By the time Abby got home, Mary had dinner ready to put on the table.

"I have my knitting group tonight," she explained, dishing up a generous dollop of tuna casserole on their plates. A salad was already on the table for them to serve themselves.

"Oh, that's right." More often than she'd like, Abby found herself so wrapped up in her own projects that she forgot to take into account Mary's busy schedule. That probably came from living so many years alone where she'd only had to keep track of herself. Of course, even then she'd often become involved in some project and forget to eat all together.

"This is our last knitting group meeting before the festival, so I'll be bringing home the sweaters and baby clothes we'll be selling there."

"Your group makes some beautiful things." Abby had taken a moment to wash up and change into comfortable jeans and a pullover top, and now she sat down at the table. "Too bad I'm hopeless when it comes to knitting or crocheting."

"You're still welcome to come to the meeting, if you'd like. We always have fun together, visiting while we work."

"I know."

Both of them bowed their heads as Mary said grace.

"But it's been a long day and I'm ready for some quiet time." Taking her first bite of casserole, Abby savored the mixed flavors of tuna, mushroom soup and curry spice, nodding her approval. "I started a new mystery novel by one of my favorite authors a week ago and didn't get very far. Maybe I can get back to that tonight."

"That's fine. I shouldn't be late getting home, and you can tell me how the story's going."

"If I'm still awake," Abby said, thinking that getting to bed early would be a good thing too.

They finished eating their meal. While Mary went off to her meeting, Abby cleaned the kitchen. After that, she sat down to watch the news on TV, most of it bad news, so she shut it off and went upstairs to her room.

With only Blossom for company, the

house was strangely quiet. Tree branches brushed against stucco; a car passed on the street, the tires humming on the asphalt. The clock on her wall ticked steadily.

Relaxing, Abby curled up in the chair next to her window and opened the mystery novel, a *New York Times* best seller that had gotten rave reviews. Flipping back a few pages from where she'd previously stopped, she caught up with the storyline and read through to the end of the next chapter.

She glanced up at her clock, and then down at her laptop sitting on her desk. The moon was about three-quarters tonight. She wondered if that would provide enough light for the hidden camera at the cove to record the scene.

She didn't really believe the suspects would try to retrieve the fake IDs at night. None of the docks were lit. Still, she couldn't resist taking one little peek to see if anything was going on.

Setting her book aside, she went to her desk and turned on her computer. With only a few clicks of the mouse, she brought up the live shot of Paradise Cove.

She drew in a sharp breath. A cabin cruiser using a spotlight was moving slowly toward the Lynches' dock. The circle of light reflected off the calm water, sweeping back and forth.

Abby grabbed her cell phone and punched in the emergency number.

"Sheriff's station. Deputy Bennett. What's your emergency?"

"This is Abby Stanton. I need to speak to Henry. Is he there?"

"I'm sorry, Dr. Stanton. The sarge went back to Lopez Island tonight."

Abby grimaced. Henry lived on Lopez. It would take him too long to get to Paradise Cove. The suspects would be gone.

"Deputy Bennett, you need to get someone out to Paradise Cove. There's a cabin cruiser there now. It's possible there are illegal aliens on board."

"Artie Washburn is on call tonight." Bennett responded quickly, apparently aware of the situation. "He'll be there as soon as he can."

"Tell him I'll meet him there."

"Ma'am, I wouldn't advise that. Those people could be dangerous."

"Just tell Artie to hurry."

Snapping her phone shut, she grabbed her jacket and a heavy-duty flashlight and ran downstairs to her car. She wasn't going to let the criminals escape if she could help it.

CHAPTER FIFTEEN

Driven by the urgency of the situation, Abby took Cross Island Road to Paradise Cove, breaking the speed limit in the process. If the cabin cruiser had illegals onboard and they discovered their expensive IDs had vanished, as a set of previous forgeries had, they'd be spooked. The counterfeiting ring would change their tactics. It'd be harder than ever to catch those at the heart of the scheme.

She killed her headlights as she reached the cove, using the moonlight to find her way to the Lynches' cabin. Parking out of sight of the dock, she got out of her car and closed the door softly. There was no sign of Artie Washburn yet or his patrol car.

As she edged her way around the cabin, her old running shoes soundless on the soft ground, she heard voices.

"It's supposed to be right there," a male voice said. "Look again, you fool."

A higher pitched female voice spoke rapidly in Spanish. She received a response from a second man in the same language.

Peering around the corner of the house, Abby had a clear view of the cabin cruiser parked at the end of the dock. The idling motor caused exhaust to cloud the air at the stern where a Canadian flag hung limply, identifying the country of registration. She strained to make out the name of the boat on the bow and its registration number.

A man lay sprawled on his stomach at the end of the dock, peering underneath much as Rick had when he and Abby found the cache originally, the Styrofoam container now tossed thoughtlessly aside. A woman stood by the boat's railing shining a flashlight toward the dock.

"Nada está aquí," the man on the dock called out. Nothing is here.

The man standing by the cabin door, presumably the boat's skipper, spoke gruffly to the couple. "Come on. Get back in the boat. I can't hang around here all day."

The other two people hurriedly spoke to each other, their Spanish too rapid for Abby to catch.

But when the man stood up on the dock ready to board the boat again, and there was still no sign of Deputy Washburn, Abby knew she had to act immediately to delay the boat's departure. She had to assume the couple were Andrea and Pablo Rodriguez there to pick up the false IDs.

Saying a quick prayer that Artie would arrive soon, she stepped out into the open and leveled her flashlight at the man on the dock. She was banking on surprise, the fact that it was dark and that they wouldn't get a good look at her. Or see that she wasn't armed.

"Everybody freeze!" she ordered in the sternest voice she could muster. "*Policía!* Police! You're all under arrest."

The man on the dock shot his arms up in the air. The woman screamed.

But the skipper ducked back into the cabin out of sight. A moment later, the inboard motor revved, churning the water.

The woman yelled at her companion on the dock. "*Venga,* Pablo! *Venga!*"

"Come! Come!"

Abby held her ground as her mind quickly translated the plea.

But the boat was already moving away from the dock. The man called Pablo glanced over his shoulder at Abby. The woman was still screaming at him and the skipper.

Out of the corner of Abby's eye, she caught the flash of red and blue lights, a patrol car arriving. *Hurry, Artie!*

Pablo panicked. Despite the fact the boat was now several feet from the dock and picking up speed, he dived into the water. His wife frantically leaned over the boat railing, her hand stretched out reaching for her husband.

A car door slammed shut and Artie came running. "Police! Stop right where you are." Gun drawn, he raced to the end of the dock.

Abby was right behind him, her jacket unzipped and flapping open. "There're two people on the boat, a woman and the boat's skipper. I'm pretty sure the woman and the man who dived off the dock are illegal aliens."

In the water, Pablo was flailing away but making little progress.

Running without lights, the boat faded into the distance as it raced for the open sea.

Eyeing the guy in the water, Artie holstered his gun. "You know if there's a life preserver around here?" he asked without looking at Abby.

"By the boathouse. I'll get it for you."

"I'd hate for that guy to drown. I don't think he can make it back to the dock, and

I'm not exactly anxious to go swimming myself."

Silently thanking the Lord that the Lynches were safety conscious, Abby raced to the boathouse. She lifted the life preserver from its hook along with the coil of rope and ran back to Artie, who was talking on his radio to Deputy Bennett at the sheriff's substation.

Artie told Bennett to stand by while he rescued the swimmer.

He heaved the life preserver within Pablo's reach and, with a little coaxing, the man grabbed hold. Artie pulled him to shore, cuffed and patted him down, then made him sit on the ground with his legs outstretched and crossed at the ankles. He began to shiver in the cool night air.

"The boat was Canadian registry," Abby told Artie when the situation seemed to be under control. "I got most of the registration number, and the name painted on the hull was *Queen III*." She gave him the digits she'd seen.

"Great. I'll ask Bennett to notify the Coast Guard. They'll pick 'em up in no time. Meanwhile, I'll get our catch-of-the-day back to the station where he can dry off. Bennett says Sarge is on his way too."

■ ■ ■ ■

Abby waited almost an hour in Henry's office while he and Artie took care of their prisoner.

When Henry joined her, he dropped into the chair behind his desk with a sigh. "I hear you took quite a risk this evening."

"I had to do something before they all got away," she explained. "I knew Artie would be there any minute."

He shook his head. "Just be glad no one on that boat decided to take a potshot at you. Probably because the skipper was in too much of a hurry to get away and didn't want to take the time."

"I am grateful." She'd already thanked the Lord that no one was hurt. "What did Pablo — if that's his name — tell you?"

"Not much so far. He's lawyered up, which means we can't get any statement from him until tomorrow when he sees his attorney. *If* he'll talk at all." Covering his mouth with his hand, Henry futilely tried to stifle a yawn. "But he was carrying a Venezuelan passport and a visa to enter Canada as well as quite a roll of cash in US dollars."

"So the counterfeit ring is bringing these people in via Canada after all."

261

"Looks like it. From Vancouver Island it's a short boat trip to Sparrow Island, then they're home free."

"Wonder how his wife feels about her husband being left behind by the skipper and then arrested by Artie."

"We'll know soon enough. A Coast Guard helicopter spotted the boat running without lights. A pursuit boat is hot on their heels and the Canadian Coast Guard is coming after them from the other direction. We should have the boat and all onboard in custody soon."

That was good. Breaking up this part of the conspiracy would probably mean no more fake IDs would be planted on Sparrow Island.

But if no one talked, they'd still be a long way from catching the ringleaders of the counterfeiting scheme.

By Wednesday morning, the story of illegal immigrants slipping into the United States via Sparrow Island and purchasing forged documents was on the front page of the weekly newspaper the *Birdcall.* At the final organizing meeting of the Best of Sparrow Island Festival committee, Donna Morgan could barely contain herself, the news was so disturbing to her.

"I'm absolutely shocked that a ring of criminals have been smuggling illegal aliens right here on Sparrow Island," she said. "I never would have guessed."

"I'm sure they intended to keep a low profile," Mary commented.

Artie Washburn nodded his agreement. "With so many foreign visitors in town, particularly during the summer, it's easy for someone to fly under the radar. We don't have any reason to suspect a stranger until something like this is uncovered."

"More than that, my business depends on tourists," Donna added. "I can't start asking people for their passports, not that I could tell a real one from a forgery anyway."

Keith Gordon leaned forward. "I'm afraid we'll have to leave this problem for the authorities to resolve. Meanwhile, I believe we should get started with the business of the day."

There appeared to be unanimous agreement all around the table.

Fortunately, the meeting went quickly. Barring any unforeseen circumstances, everything would run smoothly at the festival with one possible exception.

"My pastry chef's mother has become seriously ill," Keith reported. "She lives in Denver, so my chef's leaving today to move back there to be closer to her mother. I'm optimistic I'll be able to replace her soon. Or at least get a temporary chef hired for the weekend."

Mary plucked her second cookie of the morning from the silver serving dish. "If she's the one baking these cookies, you'll have a hard time finding anyone as talented. They're delicious."

"Be careful, Mary," Ana Dominguez warned. "I've tasted your snicker doodles, and they're extraordinary. All your desserts are. If Keith becomes desperate enough, he'll be offering you the job."

Everyone laughed, including Mary. That prospect seemed more than a little far-fetched.

After the meeting, Mary went home. She had one sweater she wanted to finish knitting before the festival and thought she'd spend the afternoon doing just that.

Her craft room was dominated by a long work table. There were ample drawers and bins for her supplies, from yarn and glitter to scissors and glue guns. Everything was easily accessible. A window provided a view of the front yard and the street beyond. Blossom particularly liked to sit on the window sill watching passing cars or birds foraging in the grass while Mary worked on her projects.

She was so engaged in her work and her thoughts, the door bell startled her. She hadn't heard anyone come up the walk and there was no car parked out front.

"Now, who do you suppose that is?" she asked Blossom, who was sitting up alertly, her ears tilted forward. Finnegan was curious, too, and came to his feet.

Guessing it might be a neighbor, Mary wheeled back from her worktable and rolled the short distance to the front door. Finnegan trotted along beside her.

"Who is it?" she called.

"It's me, Mary. Neil McDonald."

That took her by surprise. The Mc-Donalds usually came in by the back door, but perhaps Neil had knocked and she hadn't heard him.

Opening the door, she found Neil standing on the porch as well as Ileana Zeklos and young Caterina, who was grasping the kitty carrier in both her small hands.

"My, this is a pleasant surprise." She wheeled out of the way. "Please come in. Did you bring Comoară over to play with Blossom?" she asked Caterina, knowing full well Blossom wouldn't be all that thrilled at the prospect of her young feline rival reappearing in her castle.

The child's blue eyes were wide and filled with what looked like . . . fear.

Immediately, Mary knew something was terribly wrong. "What is it? What's happened?" Neil was still wearing his dark blue overalls from his ferry job, the same boat on which Ileana's husband worked. *Dear Lord, please don't let anything bad have happened to Yousef.*

They all filed into the living room behind Mary, and she turned to face them. "Tell me."

Obviously uncomfortable with what he needed to tell Mary, Neil glanced at Ileana, who looked as shaken as her daughter. "There was an immigration sweep on the ferry. They were looking for undocumented workers. They picked up Yousef."

Mary's heart sank. "But he has a green card . . ."

"It's not real." Ileana hung her head. "We tried to come legally. They would not let us."

Mary didn't know what to make of that. Her thoughts unraveled like a skein of yarn. This fine young family would surely be deported. It seemed unfair, but apparently they'd broken the law. Even so, her heart went out to them. But what could she do?

"As they were arresting Yousef," Neil said,

"he asked me to bring Ileana and their little girl to you. He thought you and Abby could help them."

But how? Mary wondered. She knew nothing about immigration laws.

"Please, Mrs. Reynolds." Holding Caterina close to her side, Ileana stroked her daughter's fine blonde hair. "If they arrest me, they will put Caterina in jail too."

Mary gasped. "They can't put a child in jail! That's unconscionable!" The mere thought of a four-year-old behind bars offended Mary's sense of right and wrong all the way to her core.

"It is true. When people come here illegally, they have few rights. That is so for the children, as well. Caterina will be detained with me. She will have nowhere to play. No toys." Ileana's chin trembled, and she smoothed the skirt of her cotton dress. "Not even her own clothes but those the jailers make her wear."

If Mary'd had a high horse, she would have climbed right on it, paralyzed or not. She was certainly there emotionally.

Her first instinct was to call Henry and ask him to prevent a terrible affront to human decency. *Putting a child in jail! Not while I still have breath left in me!* But Henry represented the law. The law, unfortunately, didn't always leave room for exceptions. She couldn't ask him to violate his own principles. Or his profession.

Knowing what she had to do, she whipped her cell phone out of the denim bag that hung in easy reach on her wheelchair and punched in Abby's number at the museum. She answered on the first ring.

"Abby, you have to come home. The Zeklos family has an emergency and needs our help. Ileana and Caterina are here with me now."

Without asking any questions, Abby's agreement came instantly. "I'll be there in fifteen minutes."

Leaning back in her chair, Mary snapped her phone shut. "Please, all of you, sit down and relax. I believe I have some chocolate chip cookies in my cookie jar. I'll make some tea for us grownups and lemonade for Caterina, and then we'll see what we can do about this fix we're in. With God's help — and Abby's — I'm sure we'll find a way out for all of you."

Tears glistened in Ileana's eyes. "Thank you," she whispered.

Once again Abby found herself speeding across Sparrow Island. She couldn't imagine what the emergency might be for the Zeklos family. It didn't matter. She'd heard the urgency in Mary's voice, and her sister was usually calm in a crisis.

She arrived home to find tension crackling in the air even as Mary served her guests. Dressed in shorts and an orange T-shirt, Caterina sat close to her mother on the silk damask couch. Looking uncomfortable, Neil McDonald stood by the fireplace holding a porcelain cup and saucer in his big, calloused hands.

"Now that Abby's here," he said, "why don't I see if Bobby's around? He can show Caterina his tree house. They can have their cookies and lemonade up there."

"An excellent idea." Mary shot Abby a concerned look. "I'll fix you a cup of tea too."

Abby nodded her thanks. It was obvious that Neil didn't want Caterina to hear what they were discussing, which meant the situation was quite serious. Her immediate thoughts flew to Yousef and his well-being. *Please, Lord . . .*

A few minutes later, Bobby showed up to whisk a reluctant Caterina out the door. Her mother spoke to her in Romanian, soft encouraging words. Finally, the child agreed to play with Bobby. The bag full of cookies and a plastic pitcher of lemonade, as well as

Bobby's gentle invitation and the promise that Finnegan could come along, gave Caterina the courage to leave her mother's side.

Left behind in her traveling cage, Comoară made her objections known.

"I'll keep an eye on the kids." Despite Neil's size and strength, the concern in his eyes made it clear he had a soft heart. "If there's anything Sandy or I can do to help, Ileana, just ask. I like Yousef. He's a good man. Things will work out, you'll see."

With a teary-eyed smile, Ileana thanked him.

Carrying her teacup, Abby sat down next to Ileana on the couch. In contrast to Ileana's simple house dress, Abby still wore the jeans and hiking boots she'd put on this morning for her final sparrow inventory.

"Now, tell me what's going on," Abby said.

The news that Yousef had been arrested was shocking enough. That was made worse by the fact that all three Zekloses were in the States with false documents. Not even visitor visas.

"Why did you feel it was so important for you to come to America that you bought counterfeit papers?" Abby asked.

Ileana visibly struggled both with her emotions and to find the right words. Her gaze darted from Abby to Mary and back again. She fingered the gold wedding band, worn on her right hand in the European style. "It was because of my father. He was a newspaperman. Very well-respected in Romania. He was proud of our country, but he knew bad things were going on."

"What sort of bad things?" Encouraging Ileana, Mary rolled her wheelchair closer to the couch.

"It was like gangs. But bigger. More like the Russian mafia. Evil people who sold drugs and paid off policemen. They make business people pay them so their stores would not be burned down. Or their families get hurt."

"Protection," Abby clarified, sick to her stomach for fear of how this story would end.

"Yes, protection." Nodding, Ileana agreed that was the word she'd been seeking. "For many in Bucharest, times were very hard because of these men. Tears, they flowed in the streets."

"We're so sorry, Ileana. We had no idea the people in Romania were having such a difficult time," Mary said.

"My father said these bad things should stop," Ileana continued. "He wrote about them in the newspaper. Many times. Ordinary people began to fight back against the gangs, not do as they were told or pay for . . . protection. That made these bad people angry."

"Good for your father for taking on those criminals," Abby said.

Ileana pulled a tissue from her pocket to wipe her eyes. "Yes, my father was very brave. Even when they threatened his life and that of my mother."

Dear Lord . . . Abby drew in a painful breath. No wonder Ileana had seemed so skittish the first time Abby met her in the meadow by Paradise Cove. Both she and her husband must have feared the mafia would pursue them all the way to America.

Mary asked the question Abby was afraid to vocalize. "Are your parents all right?"

Swallowing hard, Ileana shook her head. "One day I could not reach my mother, and my father had not gone to his office. Two days later the authorities found their bodies in a field." Unable to continue, she looked away and tried to regain her composure. "They had both been . . . tortured. The gang used my parents to send a message to those who would oppose them." She lost control then and sobbed into her hands.

Gently, Abby took the young woman in her arms, her anguish wracking her slender shoulders.

Equally touched, Mary patted Ileana's leg and crooned words of encouragement as she would have to her own child, and then offered her another tissue.

When Ileana was finally able to speak again, she said, "After my parents' funeral, when we went home, there was red paint splashed on our front door and a knife stuck in a note. It said we would be next if we did not leave the country."

"So you fled," Mary concluded.

"We tried to stay. We talked to the police, but they said they could not help us. These gangs, they are everywhere yet invisible. And then one day when I picked up Caterina at her preschool, she was crying." Again, Ileana seemed to lose her composure and fought for control. "A man had come into the school. She had her păpușă, her favorite doll, with her. The man, he took the doll's head off, threw it to the ground and stamped his foot on it."

Unable to sit still a moment longer, Abby stood and paced to the sliding glass door. Usually the view of the undulating waves beyond Mary's backyard soothed her. Not today.

She whirled. "I understand why you left Romania. I would have too." Although, God help her, except that a child was involved, she might have tried to take the law into her own hands. "But why not flee to some other European Union country? You wouldn't have needed a passport. You could have started a new life in Russia or Poland. Any number of places."

Looking up with eyes reddened by her tears, Ileana said, "We were too afraid. These bad people, they have arms that reach into all these other countries. We did go to the American embassy. Yousef pleaded with them. He tried to tell them we must come here to be safe. They listened, but said it would take time. Perhaps months. They must investigate. Be sure we are not lying." She dropped her head again. "We did not have time."

Abby felt a spurt of anger at the embassy personnel. Why hadn't they recognized how desperate the situation was for the Zekloses? Then she realized dozens, perhaps hundreds, of people apply for asylum in the United States every day from an equal number of countries. Given the requirements of Homeland Security and the continuing crises around the world, processing the requests must be an enormous task.

"If you didn't come legally, how did you find your way to America?" Mary asked.

"Yousef heard of a way. I do not know how

or where, only that it cost us a great deal of money. We had to change our names." She lifted her chin slightly. "My husband is Yousef Lazar. It is a proud name that comes from a long line of famous chefs in Romania, chefs that once served royalty. Not just cooks who make little sandwiches as Yousef must do now to support us when once he was the head chef at a big hotel where American businessmen stayed. If it had not been for me, he would not have had to give up such a large piece of his heritage."

Ah, Yousef wasn't a short-order cook, Abby realized, but a highly skilled chef.

Turning again to look out onto the ocean where the lowering sun cast streaks of diamonds across the waves, Abby prayed for a way to help Ileana and her family. They needed to get Yousef out of jail, needed the whole family to be given asylum.

But the immediate problem was to find Ileana and Caterina a place where they could be safe from detention while a way was found to let them all remain permanently in America.

The thought came to Abby as though God had sent it on the same column of golden sunshine that touched the ocean waves.

He said to them, "Let the little children come to me, and do not hinder them, for the kingdom of God belongs to such as these" (Mark 10:14).

"Little Flock Church!" she blurted out, turning away from the view and focusing on her sister and Ileana again.

Mary's brows drew together. "What are you talking about?"

"Christian churches in America have a long history of providing sanctuary to those who are escaping persecution, including those who have arrived illegally. Rev. Hale will take Ileana and Caterina in and protect them until we can work out some sort of official asylum for the whole family."

Ileana looked skeptical. "Your church would do that? Is it not against the law?"

Catching on, Mary gave Abby's proposal a nod of approval. "It's not against God's law."

"I would not want to get Rev. Hale in trouble. Or either of you. You have been most kind —"

"Don't worry about us," Abby insisted. "You take care of Caterina and yourself, and we'll find some way for your family to stay together here in America."

Granted, Abby didn't know how she'd accomplish that. But she was convinced God would guide her.

CHAPTER SIXTEEN

Before leaving the house, Abby took time to change out of her jeans and scuffed boots, and into a pair of nicer slacks and a blouse, then hurried back downstairs.

Ileana and Caterina rode in Mary's van, and Abby followed in her own car to Little Flock church. Abby was sure she'd have to make a trip to the Zekloses' cabin to pick up personal things for them. She'd probably have to see Henry Cobb as well. She needed to have her own transportation, and she hadn't wanted to appear too scruffy when she'd be asking favors of her friends.

On a Wednesday afternoon, the church parking lot was empty except for Janet Heinz's small compact, which was parked up close to the building. Rev. Hale always walked to work from his nearby parsonage.

Mary pulled into a handicapped spot, and Abby parked next to her van.

Mary and Finnegan used the lift to exit

the van. Caterina clung to her mother with one hand. In the other she carried the kitty carrier with Comoară, the child's most precious possession. She seemed determined not to leave behind another pet she loved, as she had left her dog in Romania.

Most assuredly, Caterina would not be able to keep her cat if she was sent to a detention facility with her mother.

As they all headed for the church office, Abby could tell Ileana was nervous, understandably so. Until now no one had offered to help the family except criminals who demanded payment. Abby vowed to make sure the Zekloses weren't victimized again. Or rather, the Lazars.

They all crowded into Janet's office.

"My goodness." Sitting behind her desk, Janet was obviously surprised by their arrival. With a pencil tucked behind her ear and a pile of invoices and the check register in front of her, it looked as though she'd been paying bills for the church. "Is there a meeting this afternoon I forgot?"

"Not at all," Abby said. "We're here to ask Little Flock to provide sanctuary for Ileana and her daughter until the family's approved for asylum in our country."

Janet, normally quite talkative, stared at

them blankly. "Sanctuary? I don't understand."

"Is Rev. Hale here?" Abby asked. "It might be easier if I explain to both of you what the problem is."

"He's in his office." Looking unsure, Janet stepped to the pastor's door. Her floral-print skirt flowed gracefully at midcalf length as she knocked once, opening the door when he invited her in. "Rev. Hale, we have a, um, situation here."

A moment later, he appeared. Dressed in slacks and a turtleneck sweater, he smiled warmly at the group, giving special attention to Caterina.

"What can I do for you ladies?"

Briefly, Abby explained the Lazars' status and why they'd come to Little Flock. "We believe if Ileana and Caterina are not provided sanctuary, they'll be detained by the federal authorities and will be deported back to Romania, where their lives would be at serious risk."

"I see." Despite his youthful California golden-boy good looks and outgoing personality, Rev. Hale could be serious. That was his demeanor now. "Let's talk in my office. Janet, could you find a way to occupy Caterina? Seems to me I saw her painting some pretty pictures in Vacation Bible

School the other day."

Janet eagerly jumped to the task. "I think the easel is still set up, and I know just where the smocks are kept so she won't get her pretty T-shirt dirty."

Tugging on her mother's hand, Caterina whispered something to Ileana.

"It's all right, my darling," Ileana assured her daughter. "I will take care of Comoară. You go with Mrs. Heinz."

While Janet led the child away, talking in friendly tones, Mary, Abby and Ileana preceded Rev. Hale into his office. Framed photographs of Catalina Island — the place where the pastor had grown up — as well as original oil paintings of Sparrow Island hung on the walls. On the side of the room opposite his walnut desk there was a grouping of comfortable chairs. Flowers placed on an end table next to a copy of the Bible brightened the area. The adjacent window provided a view of a stand of fir trees and the western sky.

When they were all settled, Finnegan on the floor near Mary and the cat carrier beside Ileana, the pastor leaned forward toward Ileana. He rested his forearms on his thighs, his hands clasped between his knees.

"Offering sanctuary is a very serious decision for a church to make," he said.

"I do not wish to cause you or your church trouble," Ileana said.

"I know. Tell me why you are afraid to return to Romania."

With less hesitancy this time, Ileana related the facts of her ordeal and why she and her family had left their homeland. The pastor listened attentively, nodding from time to time, and encouraging her to continue to the end of her story.

When she'd finished, he leaned back into the cushioned chair. "I'm so sorry you and your family have had such a difficult time, and for the loss of your parents. I know how hard that must have been for you, and then to have to leave your home. But I'm glad you've come to the church for help." He gazed out the window for a moment, apparently sorting through his thoughts and considering his options. "In historical terms, providing sanctuary is an ancient tradition in the Christian church. In the twentieth century, the sanctuary movement was quite active among churches during the 1980s in order to help those fleeing persecution in Central America."

"I'm not sure the Lazars fit into that category," Abby said. "The Romanian government, per se, wasn't persecuting them."

"The government certainly wasn't protecting them," Mary added. "They as much as told her she should leave the country. And our own embassy either couldn't or wouldn't help them."

Rev. Hale nodded, acknowledging the problem. "As far as I'm aware, I don't believe Little Flock has been involved in the sanctuary program in the past."

"I think it's time." Determined to help the family, Abby stated her views, perhaps too forcefully. "At least as far as the Lazars are concerned. I'm confident if the members of the church heard Ileana's story, they'd all be anxious to do whatever they could to help her and her family." She wondered if the Rodriguez couple had a similar story of persecution and hoped if they did that immigration personnel would take that into account before deporting them.

Thoughtfully, Rev. Hale folded his hands together beneath his chin in an instinctively prayerful gesture. "I think that's true. Ileana and Yousef have been here only a short time, but we already consider you both and your daughter a part of our church family."

Ileana blushed, a sheen of tears in her eyes. "Thank you, sir. Everyone has been most kind to us."

His smile was reassuring. "I'm confident

the congregation would approve of us providing your family sanctuary, Ileana. My problem is, I don't know how to proceed to get you asylum here. I'll have to research —"

"Hugo Baron knows someone in our embassy in Romania," Abby said. "I wouldn't be surprised to find that he can pull some strings to get things moving."

"I know what will help." Mary raised her hand as though she were back in school. "Keith Gordon mentioned the other day that for an immigrant to stay here permanently he'd need a sponsor, or be admitted to the country because he has a skill that's in short supply and he's been offered a job. Yousef's a skilled chef, right, Ileana?"

"Oh yes, there is nothing he cannot cook or bake. He often laughs at my efforts, but I have learned from him. I tease that if he does not cook for us, we will starve."

"The Dorset has just lost their pastry chef." Mary said. "Could Yousef make pastries and cookies?"

Pride shone in Ileana's eyes. "Like a dream. It is like his pastries, how do you say, melt in your mouth?"

Rev. Hale came to his feet. "I do believe we have a plan. Our accommodations won't be four star, Ileana, but we do have a small storage room in our recreation building that can be cleared out and will be private. Plus we have some cots and blankets on hand for an emergency. Nothing special."

"Anything will be fine. As long as my daughter and I are not sent back to Romania. And Yousef too."

The pastor held out his arms to hug the young woman. "I promise you, you'll have the prayers and good wishes of every member of Little Flock. We'll do whatever we can to provide you with a safe place to live until you and your husband receive asylum from our government."

With Ileana's agreement and instructions, Abby promised to stop by their cabin to pick up clothing and personal items for her and Caterina. She'd also ask Hugo to contact his friend in Romania. Mary said after she saw Ileana settled, she'd talk to Keith Gordon about offering Yousef a job, if he was granted asylum.

Comoară interrupted the conversation to remind everyone that she was still here. Her sharp meow startled Finnegan, who retreated a couple of steps, his toenails scrabbling on the hardwood floor.

Ileana laughed, no doubt her first light-hearted moment since Neil McDonald had told her of Yousef's arrest. "I think Como is reminding us that she will need her cat food, too, please."

Before going to the Lazars' cabin, or asking Hugo for his help, Abby decided she'd tell Henry what was going on first. Hopefully, he could find out where Yousef had been taken and if the immigration people were doing a sweep for undocumented aliens on Sparrow Island. She could well need his help to keep Matt Burns and his ICE people at bay while they worked through the process of getting asylum for the family.

When she stepped inside the sheriff's substation, she immediately realized something big was going on.

In addition to Artie Washburn behind the counter, there were two men wearing blue windbreakers that identified them as Immigration and Customs Enforcement (ICE) agents. Another half-dozen people in front of the counter were clamoring for attention, including William Jansen, editor of the *Birdcall*. Using his sharp elbows to move people out of his way, he was trying to maneuver himself to the front of the crowd.

"How many people have you detained?" he shouted toward the ICE agents. "Did those you arrested Monday night provide information that led you here to Green Harbor?"

One agent tossed a terse "No comment" over his shoulder.

"What have you done with my husband?" a woman cried out. "We're Canadian citizens. I'm going to report you to our embassy."

Another couple jostled their way into position so they could register their complaints.

Looking very much in charge, Artie held up his hand for quiet. "Please, we'll get to you as soon as we can. If you'll have a seat —"

"The public has a right to know what's going on," William insisted.

Artie nailed the editor with a stern look. "Mr. Jansen, you're interfering with police business. I suggest you move away from the counter or I'll have to lock you up too."

William hesitated a moment before turning away with a scowl on his face. His bushy eyebrows lowered into a straight line.

"The police think they can stonewall the press," he muttered, "but I'll get my story. Eventually."

"Looks like the deputies are pretty busy right now," Abby said to him. "Maybe Henry will give you a statement later."

Startled, William's head snapped around.

"Abby. I didn't see you here. What are you doing?"

"I was hoping to talk to Henry, too, but it's not looking good at the moment. I can come back later."

He eyed her suspiciously. "You know something about this illegal immigrant business, don't you? You were there when they caught that one guy Monday night." He backed her into a relatively quiet corner. "I was going to interview you for this morning's story, but the police report came in so late, I didn't have time before my deadline." He pulled a notepad from his rumpled jacket pocket and poised his pen over a blank sheet of paper. "Tell me how that arrest went down."

"I'm sure everything was in the police report." At this point, she didn't want to volunteer any information to William or anyone from the press. Certainly nothing about the Lazars and the sanctuary Little Flock was providing for the family. "Did they actually arrest some undocumented aliens today?"

"I've got reports on at least three people, but there could be more. These ICE guys have been swarming all over the dock area asking for IDs."

"Who are the three? Do you know?"

"One's a workman from the ferry. Another's an Hispanic kid working at the gas station. I guess the third's the Canadian that woman's been screaming about." He indicated the woman wearing slacks and a sleeveless blouse who had asked about her husband.

Abby guessed the detained ferry worker was Yousef. "How long are they going to keep the detainees here?"

"Not long, I imagine. No more than a day or two. Then they'll take them to a detention center at Bellingham, where they'll hold them until there's a hearing."

"How long will that take?"

"If they appeal or request asylum, they're looking at being locked up for a couple of months." He tilted his head to the side. "You sure are curious about these illegals. I thought you just happened to be at Paradise Cove when the guy was plucked out of the water. But it's more than that, isn't it?"

Abby tried to play innocent. But despite a relatively short career as a newspaperman, just since he'd purchased the *Birdcall* five years ago, William had demonstrated he had a nose for news.

"For now, I'm going to say 'no comment,' I'm afraid. Maybe later I'll be able to fill you in on the details."

"Now, Abby," he cajoled. "You can't leave me hanging like that. I want a follow-up story in next week's edition."

"Sorry, William." She glanced around at the agitated people in the lobby area. "I'll come back later to talk to Henry when he's not so busy." She'd try to get him to keep Yousef here on Sparrow Island while they pursued asylum, but she wasn't sure he had the authority to do that when the feds were involved.

Hugo was next on her list.

The Nature Museum was still open when Abby arrived. She waved to Wilma as she went inside and hurried through the door to the offices. When she didn't find Hugo in his office, she felt a surge of anxiety. There was no time to waste. The wheels of government worked slowly at best. Worst case, the wheels were brought to a grinding halt by unwieldy rules and government bureaucracy.

She exhaled in relief when she found Hugo in the laboratory peering through their high-powered microscope.

"Sorry to interrupt," she said as she entered the room.

Hugo looked up from the microscope. "Not a problem. I was just examining some old seeds I gathered in Kenya and comparing them to samples of similar plants I gathered here. Is there something I can do for you?"

She perched herself on one of the high stools at the lab table. "I'm afraid I need a very big favor."

He arched his brows. "Name it."

"It's about the Romanian family I told you about, the one that's been living at Paradise Cove."

He listened intently as she described the situation, finally taking notes on a yellow legal pad he found in one of the lab table drawers.

On the counter, an incubator for hatching eggs and a box for brooding newly hatched chicks stood empty. The most dangerous part of the season was over. Soon the last of the bald eagles born this spring would fledge, although they'd stay close to home for a year or more.

Abby hoped that Ileana, Yousef and Caterina would be safely in their own home with the proper documentation before that.

"I'm hoping you can get your friend at our embassy in Bucharest to expedite their request for asylum here," Abby concluded.

Hugo hastily scribbled some more notes in his flourishing handwriting. "You say their real name is Lazar?"

"Yes." She spelled it for him. "They used a false name on their forged documents hoping that the Romanian gangsters wouldn't be able to track them down. You'll have to ask your friend to be discreet. We don't want their local mafia showing up here in Green Harbor."

Nodding, Hugo glanced at his watch, an expensive model with a wide silver band. "Given the time difference, it's the middle of the night in Bucharest now. I'll give him a call in a few hours and see if he can get things moving from his end. I also have an acquaintance in the State Department in Washington, DC, an old climbing partner. He may be able to assist us. I'll call him in the morning."

Unable to help herself, Abby chuckled. "Is there any influential person in this country you don't know?"

"Perhaps one or two," he said with mock modesty and a twinkle in his deep blue eyes.

Mary made sure Ileana and her daughter would be reasonably comfortable sleeping in the small storage room at the church. It seemed a dreadful place to Mary, only one small window, but Ileana seemed relieved to have a place where she and Caterina were safe, and the child would have the entire recreation room as her playground. Ileana's fear of being forced to return to Romania was palpable.

Knowing Abby would pick up clothes and necessities for Ileana and her daughter, Mary drove across the island to the Dorset to enlist Keith Gordon's help.

One of the bell boys escorted her back to Keith's office.

"How badly do you need a pastry chef?" she asked as she wheeled herself into his spacious office.

"Name your price, Mary, and you're hired!"

She laughed. That wasn't at all what she'd meant.

"You flatter me, Keith. Truth is, I couldn't possibly keep up with the pressures of a commercial establishment."

He came around to her side of the desk and took her hands. "My dear, I'm confident we could make accommodations for you and your exquisite abilities, but I sense that's not why you're here."

"Very perceptive of you, Keith." Squeezing his hands, she felt gratified by his reaction. "Let me tell you about a wonderful chef I know, one who would be a great asset to the Dorset."

As she explained Yousef's situation, Keith

pulled up a chair to sit next to her, listening to her tale.

When she finished, he said, "Tell me more about this man's credentials as a chef."

"I'm not quite sure other than he was the head chef at a hotel where Americans stayed. But I'm confident you'd find him a wonderful, hardworking employee. If you can offer him a job, I think we'll have a good chance of getting him the political asylum he and his family need."

Bending his head, Keith seemed to weigh Mary's recommendations. When he looked up, he said, "Bring me more about his experience. I'll do what I can. And I certainly can use his skill, if it's as strong as you suggest."

Mary promised to bring him whatever information he needed.

CHAPTER SEVENTEEN

After talking with Hugo, Abby visited the Lazars' cabin at Paradise Cove, using Ileana's key to let herself in. Neat as the proverbial pin, it was eerily quiet. Children's books in both English and Romanian were stacked on an end table. The pillows on the couch were fluffed as though Ileana had expected company.

Abby stood for a moment silently admiring the bronze crucifix on the wall. Deeply touched that this exquisite piece of art, a powerful symbol of the family's faith, was one of the few possessions the Lazars had brought from their homeland, she began to pray.

"Dear Lord, please help us find a way to keep Ileana, Yousef and Caterina, Your servants, safe in America. They have shown themselves loving and faithful to Your teachings and seek refuge in Your embrace. Amen."

Feeling relieved now that she'd turned the burden of the Lazars' fate over to the Lord, she turned to the task at hand. She found the suitcase in the closet, as Ileana had told her, and began to select clothing and personal items that would see them through at least a few days at the church. If necessary, she could return later for anything she'd forgotten.

In the kitchen, she noticed a large bowl filled with at least three dozen of Ileana's exquisitely decorated rocks — many more than she'd seen previously. Ileana had clearly been working hard in the hope of bringing in a bit of extra money for her family.

Abby hoped Ileana's efforts would pay off, although she doubted asylum could be arranged that quickly even with Hugo's influence. Until it was, Ileana couldn't risk leaving the sanctuary of the church for fear the federal authorities would arrest her and Caterina.

With the suitcases and Como's box of cat food safely in her car, Abby headed back to the sheriff's substation. Though it was almost dinner time, the June sun was still well above the horizon. A cool sea breeze fluttered the colorful banners hanging from light posts along Municipal Street that announced the upcoming Best of Sparrow Island Festival.

She was gratified to find no one mobbing the counter at the sheriff's office and was equally confident Artie was pleased the place had cleared out.

"Looks like business has slowed down," she said as she approached the counter.

He grinned lopsidedly. "The sarge had to get pretty tough with 'em, especially William Jansen."

"I can imagine. Our newspaper's editor-in-chief can be a very determined man. Is Henry still around?"

"Yeah, he's in the back with Agent Burns."

"How about the people who were arrested? Are they still in custody here?"

"Yep. We pretty much have a full house back there." He lifted his chin toward the two jail cells at the back of the building. "I'm gonna fix 'em up with supper in a bit. I think Agent Burns is planning to transport the detainees to Bellingham in the morning."

Relieved to hear Yousef was still on the island, Abby was also concerned that he'd be sent to the mainland as soon as tomorrow. That didn't give her much time to convince Henry to use his influence to retain custody of Yousef.

"I'd really like to talk with Henry," she said. "Tell him it's important."

"I'll try. But that ICE agent has had him tied up for hours."

"Then maybe he'll be glad for a break."

Using the intercom, Artie called Henry, who seemed reluctant to break up his meeting with the federal agent. Finally, he grudgingly agreed.

When he appeared, Abby noted the taut lines around Henry's eyes and the firm set to his lips, the signs of a stressful afternoon.

"I'm sorry to bother you, Henry."

"Abby, I'm really busy. Unless you've got a crisis, I'd really appreciate —"

"It's about Yousef Zeklos and his family," she said, using the name that was familiar to Henry. "Little Flock is giving his wife and daughter sanctuary, and the family intends to request political asylum here in the States."

Henry's eyes narrowed. "You're telling me Rev. Hale is harboring undocumented aliens in the church?"

"Providing *sanctuary*," she emphasized. "Once you hear their harrowing story, you'll understand why."

Rubbing his palm over his face, he shook his head. "Yousef has been totally close-mouthed about his situation. Hasn't said word one. No way will he get asylum if he doesn't open up to Agent Burns about how he got those forged documents."

"Maybe he's afraid of what will happen to his wife and child. That they'll be sent back to Romania and their lives will be in danger, if he talks. If he knows they're safe, maybe then he'll open up to you."

"I don't know, Abby . . ."

"Let me talk to him. He might not believe you, but I can reassure Yousef his family's safe. You and Agent Burns can be present."

After a moment's hesitation, Henry relented, warning that Agent Burns would have the last word.

Abby waited in a small interrogation room while Henry explained the situation to Matt Burns and fetched Yousef from his cell. The room contained a metal table and four straight-back chairs that had probably been bought when the substation was built in the 1950s. Comfort had not been a consideration, and the pale green walls suggested that hiring an interior decorator had not been an issue, either. Along with the faint scent of disinfectant, there was an overpowering sense of isolation in the room.

Abby thought if she was forced to spend too many hours alone in the room, she'd be ready to confess to almost anything in order to get out.

When the door opened, she stood.

With his wrists cuffed together behind his back and wearing an orange prison jumpsuit, Yousef was ushered inside. His hazel eyes flared when he saw her and they were filled with both fear and pleading.

"Your wife and daughter are safe, Yousef," she said. "Mary and I took them to Little Flock Church, which has given them sanctuary. They'll be fine until we can get this situation worked out."

The tortured look in his eyes eased. "Thank you."

Henry unlocked his handcuffs, gesturing for Yousef to sit down.

Agent Burns, dressed in a blue suit, glowered at Abby. "What you and your friends are doing regarding this sanctuary business could get you in serious trouble, Dr. Stanton. You're walking a dangerous line."

"In this case, we think we're on God's side of the line, Agent Burns. We're doing everything we can to help Yousef and his family gain political asylum."

Still scowling, he folded his arms across his chest. "This man is in the country illegally and had forged documents in his possession. He's a criminal just like the rest of them."

Henry pulled out a chair for himself. "Sit down, Abby. Matt. Let's talk."

Abby did as the sergeant suggested, but Agent Burns continued to stand, apparently determined to maintain the power position.

"Yousef, the best way for you to help yourself and your family," Henry said, "is to tell us how you acquired those fake documents. I don't know if you'll be offered asylum in this country if you come clean. But I'm confident that if you *don't* tell everything you know about the counterfeit ring, you'll be going back to Romania. No one can offer you protection there."

His hands resting flat on the table, Yousef slanted Abby a pleading look.

She covered his hand with hers. "Tell them what you know. In this day and age, there are dangerous people who would use the same high-quality fake documents you used to get into the country in order to harm the United States. You're not one of those people. Sergeant Cobb and Agent Burns know that as well as I do. But you have to help us protect ourselves from people who are just as evil as the gangsters who killed Ileana's parents."

His hand folded into a fist. "Can you promise me that Ileana and our little girl will be safe?"

Abby had always made it a point not to promise what she couldn't guarantee, and she swallowed hard before she spoke. So much about this situation was out of her control — how the governments of two countries might react to the situation, whether the news of the Lazars' escape to America would raise the ire of the Romanian gang, whether the counterfeiters might take revenge on Yousef's family if he spoke up.

She squeezed his hand one more time. "I swear I will do everything in my power to keep your family safe and so will the members of Little Flock Church. I believe God brought you to us and Sparrow Island for a reason, and that He wants you to fulfill that purpose here with us. You need to have the faith and strength to believe that too."

He studied her for a long moment before nodding. "Very well. I will tell them what I know."

Exhaling, Abby prayed that she'd done the right thing by encouraging Yousef to speak out, that the Lord would protect both him and his family from harm.

Henry placed a tape recorder on the table and turned it on. "All right, let's start at the beginning. How did you first make contact

301

with the people that provided the counterfeit documents?"

Taking a deep breath, Yousef began. "There is a man in Bucharest who used to provide documents for those who wished to move to other countries in Europe. That was before there was a European Union, which made immigration from one country to another much easier. I went to him asking for help."

"Let's have the guy's name," Burns ordered.

Yousef told him, then continued. "This man said he could get us visas to visit Canada. Once there, I was to send a letter to a post office box in New Jersey along with small photographs of my family and the money to buy new documents."

He named an amount that must have represented a year's worth of income for Yousef in Romania.

Burns asked for the name he sent the letter to and address, which Yousef provided.

"I was also to tell this person my e-mail address, which I was to arrange at an Internet coffee shop or some other public place. After that I was to wait for further instructions."

"How long was it before you heard from these people?" Henry asked.

"It took more than a week. I was getting very nervous. I had sent them almost all of the money Ileana and I had saved. Soon I would not be able to pay for the room we rented or the food we ate."

"That must have been the time it took to create the documents and get them to their contact here on Sparrow Island," Abby concluded.

"In the e-mail they gave me the name of a boat captain who would bring us to the United States and give us our papers."

Agent Burns named the skipper of the *Queen III.* "Was that the guy?" he asked.

"Yes." Anger flickered briefly in Yousef's eyes. "Once we were out of the Victoria marina on Vancouver Island, he asked for more money, which I did not expect. When I could not pay him what he wanted, he threatened to throw Caterina overboard." Lowering his head, he studied the marred tabletop, running a fingertip along the length of a scratch mark. "Ileana had a diamond ring that had been her mother's. He made her give it to him. I could not stop him."

Deep inside, Abby felt a surge of anger. What a cruel thing to do to people who were desperate. "Agent Burns already has that skipper locked up. Personally, I hope he throws away the key."

"I'll do my best," Matt said, looking as grim as Abby felt.

"Did the boat captain know where the documents were hidden?" Henry asked.

"Yes, I think so. He seemed to check his navigation system carefully. But when we reached Paradise Cove, he knew where I should look. Under one of the docks."

"Sounds like one of Remijio Bejos' favorite hiding spots," Abby commented. "Remi must have contacted the skipper of the boat after he planted the documents at the geocaching site. To anyone overhearing a phone conversation or reading an e-mail, the exchange of information would seem innocent." Which meant one of her earlier assumptions had been wrong. It wasn't the illegal immigrant who checked the geocaching Web site; it was the skipper of the boat, and he'd learned which site to visit based on contact with Remi or some other individual who actually hid the forged IDs. There could actually be more than one person like Remi involved.

"Did you ever post any messages on a geocaching Web site?" she finally asked, still puzzling over how the system worked.

Nodding, Yousef said, "One time. I used

the library computer here on the island the day after we arrived. I had been told what to do and what I should say using my screen name again."

"That's how you told them you had received your papers."

"That is so."

"Let's go back a bit. What happened right after you found the documents?" Burns asked.

Yousef shrugged. "He put us off the boat with our suitcases, and we walked into town. The next day we asked at the Visitors Center. They arranged that we stay in the cabin at the cove, and with my green card, I got a job on the ferry."

"But not with your real name," Abby said softly.

His head snapped around. "Ileana told you?"

"Yes, and she told us you're a fine chef, Yousef Lazar. We're trying to get you a job at the Dorset and we've asked the owner of the hotel to sponsor you."

Henry looked surprised. "Keith Gordon's going to do that?"

"Mary's working on it," Abby said.

"Sounds to me like everybody's gone soft on this island," Burns mumbled, apparently not pleased that the community had come to Yousef's defense.

Abby's lips curled into a smile. "We think the Lazar family will make a fine addition to our town and we look forward to the day when they become full-fledged citizens of the United States."

Visibly struggling against the emotion he was feeling, Yousef said, "My wife and I would like that very much. It is our dream to make our home here."

As Abby looked up at a scowling Agent Burns, she prayed that he and the government he represented would allow Yousef's dream to come true.

Burns asked for a few more details; Yousef's answers were forthright.

When the agent's interrogation ran out of steam, Abby said, "I'm hoping you'll either release Yousef in my custody or allow him to remain here under Sergeant Cobb's supervision while we work out the details of asylum for the Lazar family, rather than detaining him in Bellingham."

"You've got to be kidding!" Burns speared his fingers through his closely cropped hair, and his five o'clock shadow seemed to darken with his angry mood. "The man's a criminal. He's in the country illegally. Can't you people get that through your heads? There are procedures, proper ways of doing things. He can request asylum once he's *detained,* not before."

With quiet calm, Abby said, "As it happens, he already requested asylum from our embassy in Bucharest."

"And the embassy turned him down!" Burns said.

"Not at all. They did, however, inform him the process would be a long one. Because of the imminent danger they faced, the Lazar family wisely decided to come on their own to the States and wait out the bureaucratic red tape in safety. I have confidence in their statement of the facts, and I'm sure asylum will be approved."

Burns looked like he wanted to object, but was too upset to find the right words.

"I can get that immigration attorney who represented the kid from Belize back here in the morning," Henry volunteered. "Personally, I have no problem retaining custody of Mr. Lazar."

"Thank you, Henry."

Burns drew himself up to his full six feet. "This is very irregular. I'll have to clear this with my superior."

Standing, Abby momentarily placed a reassuring hand on Yousef's shoulder. "We appreciate your being flexible, Agent Burns. When you explain to your supervisor how the citizens of Green Harbor feel about the Lazars, I'm sure he'll be willing to make an exception in this case."

Burns didn't look convinced.

"Meanwhile," Abby added, "I picked up some of Ileana and Caterina's things from their cabin. I'll take them to the church and see that Yousef's family is well taken care of."

Yousef quietly expressed his thanks before Henry took him back to his jail cell.

Agent Burns gave a disbelieving shake of his head. "I'll get our people in New Jersey tracking down the counterfeiting ringleaders there. The information Yousef provided about the PO box — which should get us an address of the box owner — and his contact in Romania, plus what we can drag out of the boat's skipper, will help us nail them. And we're tracking down the Internet provider's leads. But that doesn't mean Lazar won't be deported like any other illegal alien who's committed a felony."

The good Lord was going to have to work on opening both Matt Burns's heart and his mind, Abby thought as she returned to her car.

High-pitched giggles echoed around the recreation room at Little Flock Church.

A ping-pong game of sorts was in progress when Abby arrived. Although the ping-pong table was set up, the rules appeared newly invented. Ileana served the ball over the net. Caterina, too young to successfully hit it back, missed the ball, which then bounced wildly on the hard linoleum floor. That resulted in a spirited race between Caterina and Comoară under and around tables and chairs to see who would get to the ball first.

Meanwhile, Ileana and Mary, who had returned from the Dorset, cheered the playful duo on with their laughter.

Their good spirits lifted Abby's heart as she set the two suitcases down near the door of the storage room. Inside, two cots were already made up and ready for Ileana and Caterina.

"That looks like a game designed to wear out both child and cat," Abby commented.

Laughing, Mary said, "It's certainly wearing me out. My stomach muscles ache from laughing."

With a suddenly sober expression, Ileana asked, "What of my husband? Do you know where he is? Is he all right?"

"He's fine," Abby hastened to assure her. "He's at the sheriff's substation here on the island. With any luck, he'll remain there until your situation can be worked out and asylum is granted."

Tears of relief glistened in Ileana's blue eyes, and she wiped them away with the heels of her hands.

"Mama, Mama!" Worried by the tears, Caterina raced to her mother's side and spoke rapidly in Romanian. In response, Ileana squatted down to the child's level and reassured her everything would be all right.

When the child seemed calm, Abby told of her meeting with Hugo and the calls he'd be making to Bucharest and the State Department in Washington, DC.

Mary reported her success with Keith Gordon, garnering his promise to hire Yousef as soon as he could provide a resumé and his immigrant status was approved.

With that good news shared, Mary announced that Patricia Hale, the pastor's wife, had brought them spaghetti and a salad for dinner and promised to bring her son Toby over in the morning to play with Caterina.

"We have so much to be thankful for — you two and all your friends," Ileana said. "I do not know how we will ever thank you properly."

Abby gave her a quick hug. "The relief I saw on Yousef's face when he knew you were all right and the laughter I heard when I came in the door here is enough thanks for me."

"Any thanks for what we're doing belongs to the Lord, not us," Mary said. "His heart rejoices at the sound of a child's laughter too."

CHAPTER EIGHTEEN

The following morning, Abby made it a point to get to the museum early. She found Hugo had beaten her there and was already at his desk dressed for his workday in a classic tan summer suit with narrow lapels.

"I spoke with my friend's son at the embassy in Bucharest last night," Hugo said. "I have to say the news was a bit troubling."

"That doesn't sound good." She sat down heavily in the leather guest chair in front of Hugo's desk, and idly smoothed her khaki skirt over her knees. "What did you find out?"

He glanced down at the yellow legal pad where he'd been making notes. "My contact was aware of the Lazars' situation. At the time they requested asylum, there were apparently some political ramifications that made the State Department uncomfortable."

"Like the local mafia was applying pressure?"

"He wasn't specific about the problem. I gathered the situation was sufficiently sensitive that the details remained hush-hush."

With a discouraged sigh, Abby leaned back, the leather chair embracing her. "So he doesn't think he can help us?"

"He indicated he'd look into the matter, which is bureaucratese for not wanting to stick his neck out too far. However, if he's anything like his father, he'll do his best for us."

"It'd be criminal if Yousef and his family were deported to Romania where their lives could still be in danger."

"We must not give up so easily. My friend at the State Department in Washington, DC is pursuing the situation from his end as well. He may be in a better position to affect the outcome of the Lazar request via his own high-level contacts than my man in Bucharest. He's farther away from the Romanian political influence."

"Let's hope so. Last night, Yousef told Henry and the immigration agent how he contacted the counterfeiters via a post office box. When someone rents a PO box, they have to list an address, which should be a good lead for the authorities to follow.

I'm hoping Yousef's cooperation will help expedite his request for asylum."

"Very possibly. He may eventually have to testify as well."

"I'm sure he'd do that if he was assured his family would be safe."

"Understandable." Leaning back, Hugo tented his fingers under his chin. "Now that the wheels are set in motion, all we can do is wait."

"That's the hard part." Although Abby had always had plenty of patience when it came to observing birds in their natural habitat, her forbearance was much shorter when it came to helping her friends.

The answers will come in God's time, she reminded herself, though she couldn't help but wish He'd move quickly, for the sake of the Lazar family.

She'd just barely hung up her lightweight blazer in her own office when her phone rang. It was Henry.

"Agent Burns says both Yousef and Ileana have to fill out some government immigration form, a USCIS Form I-589," Henry said.

"That sounds typical of our government. Forms come first."

"Then they can meet with a hearing officer. I can handle that for Yousef if you can get the form to Ileana."

"Sure, I can do that. Where do I get the form?"

"It's downloadable on the Internet." He gave her the Web site information. "I recommend she meet with the hearing officer at the church, otherwise she'll lose the sanctuary protection Little Flock is providing."

"I'll pass that information along. When do you suppose she'll have her hearing?"

He didn't respond immediately, and she heard conversation in the background, a male voice.

"Burns can't promise any sooner than a hundred and twenty days," Henry said.

Four months? Assuming they're granted asylum at all.

Poor Yousef and Ileana, their family separated, him confined behind bars and Ileana restricted to the church and its grounds with her daughter.

For some, immigration to the United States carried a high price tag.

By midmorning, Mary had loaded the boxes of completed baby sweaters and caps from her knitting group into her van, which she'd parked in the driveway for easier access. Although the festival didn't officially begin until Saturday, she wanted to have everything ready to set up tomorrow. That meant she had to go by Island Blooms to load Candace's wreaths today as well.

Aaron's woodworkers and Goldie Landon, with her exquisite orchids, were providing their own transportation.

Meanwhile, she'd promised to get Yousef's resumé to Keith Gordon. Since he wasn't likely to have his resumé with him in jail, that might be a problem. She also needed to pick up Ileana's decorative rocks for the festival, something the young woman couldn't do herself without risking arrest for immigration violations.

Mary glanced up at the sky, a clear blue bisected by a single white contrail silently tracking the path of an airplane no larger than a speck of dust.

"Lord, I'm going to need Your help to get me through this day and all I have to do. Either that, or I'll need a new set of legs."

"Mary! Mary!" Bobby came dashing across the lawn from the neighboring yard. "Whatcha doing?"

Finnegan, who had been patiently waiting nearby, wagged his tail in welcome as the ten-year-old hurried toward them.

Laughing, Mary opened her arms and let Bobby run into them for a hug. "Bobby Mc-Donald, I do believe you and your strong legs have been sent by God. How would you like to help me with my errands today?"

He grinned, his hazel eyes, framed by dark lashes, sparkled with youthful enthusiasm. "Sure. I gotta ask Mom though."

"You do that. Tell her I'll take good care of you, and maybe even feed you lunch at Springhouse Café."

"Cool." Racing back to his house, Bobby's feet seemed to fly over the ground. Within moments, he reappeared and his mother stepped out onto their front porch.

"Thanks for the loan of your son," Mary called, waving to Sandy. "I won't keep him long."

"Just have him back in time for the start of school in the fall."

Laughing, Mary remembered how trying the first few days and weeks of summer vacation had been for her before Zack and Nancy settled into the relaxed routine of their long holiday.

Once in the van and buckled up, Bobby asked, "So what are we gonna do?"

"First we're going by the church." Mary made sure Finnegan was secure, then snapped her chair into place. "I need to talk with Ileana Lazar, Caterina's mother."

"I helped out at Vacation Bible School last week. Caterina's English was getting better every day."

"Good for you for helping at church." She backed out of the driveway and headed toward Harbor Seal Road. "How's the fishing contest going?"

"Not good," he grumbled. "Dad always has to work long hours during the summer. You know, crew members take vacations and he has to fill in and stuff. But he's promised we can go fishing first thing Saturday morning, rain or shine."

"Well, I certainly hope you catch a big one this time."

"Yeah, me too."

Within a few minutes, Mary pulled into the church parking lot and discovered Abby's car was there.

"Looks like Ileana is getting lots of company this morning," Mary commented as Bobby helped push her chair into the recreation building.

They discovered Ileana, Abby and Janet Heinz sitting around the ping-pong table, using it as a writing table. Caterina was playing nearby with some toys from the preschool classroom.

"Looks like we all had the same idea to visit Ileana," Mary said.

The women greeted each other while Caterina got reacquainted with Finnegan and

Bobby supervised the younger child. Ileana reported she and her daughter had slept well enough on the cots, and Janet had brought them rolls, cheese and salami for breakfast along with milk for Caterina.

"Caterina missed her father and the doll she sleeps with at night," Ileana said. "I promised her she would have her papa and her doll back soon."

"We're all hoping for that," Janet said.

"I brought Ileana some immigration forms to fill out," Abby explained.

"America requires much paperwork." Ileana indicated the several sheets of paper that were in front of her. "As does my government, I am sure."

"I need a bit of paperwork too," Mary said. "Keith Gordon at the Dorset needs Yousef's work history. I'm hoping you have his resumé at the cabin. If you do, then Bobby and I can fetch it."

"This Mr. Gordon will hire my Yousef?"

"As soon as his papers are in order," Mary assured her.

"Yousef will be so happy. I wish I could tell him the good news."

"It may be a while before you can see him," Abby said. "The federal agent said it could be as long as four months before your hearing."

Ileana looked stunned. "That long?"

Janet hooked her wrist on her hip. "That's ridiculous. Surely the government doesn't keep people in limbo for such a long time. Keep families apart like that? It's criminal."

"I'm really sorry, Ileana," Abby said. "We'll keep working to shorten the time period. For now, if you write Yousef a note, I'll be happy to deliver it to him when I return these forms to the sheriff's office."

"Yes, I would like that." From her expression, Ileana clearly felt corresponding with her husband behind bars was a far cry from actually seeing him.

She switched her attention back to Mary. "Yousef did write up his work history, a resumé as you say, but he was afraid to use it when he asked for the job on the ferry. So he just made himself a cook on the application form." She shook her head. "We have had to say so many lies."

Janet took her hand and patted it kindly. "You've got us and the Lord on your side now. You won't have to lie any more."

"We are very lucky, and you have been most kind. All of you."

"Is the resumé at your cabin?" Mary asked.

"Yes. It is in Yousef's small briefcase in our bedroom."

"Good. With your permission, Bobby and I will go by your cabin and pick up the resumé and your painted rocks for the festival. I'm loading up my van with everything I have to take tomorrow for the setup."

"Mary, I don't think Ileana's cabin is wheelchair accessible," Abby warned. "The walkway's uneven, and there are a couple of steps to get inside."

Smiling smugly, Mary said, "That's why I brought Bobby along. He's going to be my legs today."

After leaving the church, Mary drove to Island Blooms where Candace and Bobby loaded the wreaths of dried flowers into the van. Then they headed to Paradise Cove.

"I guess if you weren't born here," Bobby said, "it's hard to become an American."

"It's not easy," Mary agreed. "But thousands of people become naturalized citizens every year."

"But they can't become president of the United States, and I can."

Pausing to let some tourists jaywalk across Shoreline Drive, she slanted him a look. "Are you planning to run for president?"

He shrugged. "Maybe. After I've become an astronaut and go into outer space."

"Ah." Looking away, she stifled a laugh.

Bobby was so smart, and often determined when he set a goal for himself, he just might do both.

She parked on the road in front of the Lazars' cabin.

"Here's the key, Bobby. Mrs. Lazar said the briefcase is in the bedroom near their dresser. If you'll bring it to me, I'll see if I can find Yousef's resumé." She didn't like the idea of snooping through someone else's private papers, but there didn't seem to be any other choice in this case.

Finnegan remained with Mary, alertly watching out the window for Bobby's return.

It didn't take long. "Is this it?" he asked, hopping back into the van with the briefcase Ileana had described.

"Looks like it to me." She found the one-page resumé easily, slipped it out and handed the briefcase back to Bobby. "Now for the rocks. They're in the kitchen. But if they're too heavy for you, divide them up and make two trips."

"I'll be careful, Mary. Honest."

She smiled as he raced back into the cottage. Did the boy ever move slowly? She wondered. Probably not.

Minutes later, with Ileana's artistically decorated rocks safely in the van along with

Caterina's favorite doll that Bobby had thoughtfully remembered, Mary drove to the Dorset.

The desk clerk escorted her and Bobby to Keith's office. Sunlight streaked in through the window, glancing off a section of dark wood wainscoting, repeating the rectangular pattern of the window frame in light and shadow.

"What a delightful surprise, Mary." Keith took both of Mary's hands in his first, then shook hands with Bobby. "Master Mc-Donald, I believe."

Standing soldier straight, Bobby grinned. "Yes, sir. I'm helping Mary today."

"Good for you, young man." Keith sat on the corner of his desk. "How may I assist you today, Mary?"

"I have Yousef's resumé." She handed him a single sheet of paper. "From the looks of it, Yousef has had some very responsible positions in some top-notch kitchens. I'm sure he'll be an asset to the Dorset."

Taking a moment, Keith scanned Yousef's work experience. "Yes, quite an impressive record."

"According to his wife, Yousef's family has a long history of producing top chefs in Romania."

"Then I will be more than happy to have

him on my payroll. When will his papers be in order so that he can start work?"

"That may be a bit of a problem." Anxiously, she tapped her fingers on the armrest of her wheelchair. "There has to be a hearing on his request for asylum. According to the immigration people, the wait could be as long as four months."

Keith remained silent for a long moment, then set the resumé aside on his desk. "That's a serious problem, I'm afraid. I'm going to have to hire a permanent pastry chef soon. In four months, we'll be past the busiest part of the tourist season. I generally start cutting back on staff about then. Hiring new staff so late in the year . . ." He shook his head. "I simply couldn't justify that, Mary. I'm sorry."

"I understand, Keith. We'll just have to hope and pray the powers that be decide to move quickly for a change."

She felt heartsick. One thread of the plan that would allow Yousef and his family to stay in America was unraveling. If the rest of the fabric came apart, if the government disallowed the Lazars' request for asylum, then they'd be put in the untenable position of having to return to Romania.

Mary decided both she and the Lazars would have to rely on the lesson taught in the Book of Job: "But if it were I, I would appeal to God; I would lay my cause before him" (Job 5:8).

CHAPTER NINETEEN

On Saturday morning, Abby stopped by the church to visit Ileana. Unfortunately, she had no news to report about the Lazars' asylum request and probably wouldn't have for months. But it was way too soon to become discouraged.

After that, she went on to the Best of Sparrow Island Festival. By the time she arrived at the Dorset, the crowd had begun to build.

As she was strolling across the grounds, she spotted Wilma Washburn talking with a young woman in front of the basket display. Today the museum secretary was wearing a traditional Native American dress made of buckskin and decorated with colorful beads and feathers. She'd pulled her gray hair into two long braids.

"Good morning, Wilma. Looks as though your friends came through with a lot of handwoven baskets to sell."

"They did indeed. And they're all beautifully unique." Understandable pride shone in her dark eyes. "Abby, I'd like you to meet Ashley Tomlins. She's the young lady who lives on San Juan Island that I told you about. She's just learning to do basket weaving." Wilma slipped her arm around Ashley's shoulders and gave her a motherly hug.

The teenager smiled shyly. Her mixed racial background had given her a light olive complexion, dark hair and exotic eyes that would some day make her a striking woman. "I'm afraid I'm not very good yet, but Wilma says she'll teach me."

"I admire anyone who even attempts basket weaving." Abby held out her hands palms up. "I'm afraid I'm all thumbs when it comes to almost any craft."

"Actually, for a first effort, Ashley's baskets are quite good." Wilma picked up a middle-sized basket, one that she'd shown Abby at the museum. "I think, in time, she'll be a very talented weaver and her baskets will be in great demand."

Abby took the basket from her and traced the careful zigzag pattern of the weave. "You know what? If you say Ashley's going to be a popular weaver, I should get in on the ground floor. How much are you asking for this basket?"

Startled, Ashley stammered a price that might well have been too high under other circumstances. But it was a perfect investment in a young woman's future and a boost to her self-confidence.

But knowing the ways of the Native culture, Abby bargained her down a dollar or two so they'd both feel that they'd made a good deal. Wilma beamed her approval when they concluded the sale.

Proudly carrying her purchase, Abby went in search of the geocaching display where Rick DeBow was handling the first shift at the festival. She found him chatting with her mother behind the table they shared.

"Have you convinced Mother to take up geocaching yet?"

Ellen Stanton laughed. "I'm afraid my days of tramping through the woods have long passed, although I admit the treasure hunting idea is intriguing."

"There're lots of caches that are easy to reach, Mrs. Stanton, even some that are right alongside a road," Rick pointed out. "Others are no more than an excuse to take in a particularly nice view another cacher has enjoyed."

Eyes twinkling with amusement, Helen said, "I'll say this, you make a persuasive case for the hobby."

Abby's cell phone sounded. Pulling it from the holster at her belt, she checked the caller's number.

"Hi, Henry. What's up?"

"There's been a jail break."

Her eyes widened. "A what?" Surely she hadn't heard him correctly.

"Yousef broke out of jail. More than an hour ago, a man came into the station and caught Deputy Bennett off guard. Pistol whipped him, knocked him unconscious and trussed him up like a Christmas goose. Then he let Yousef out of his cell and the two of them took off. The medics took Bennett to the Medical Center. They say he'll be okay."

Nearly speechless, Abby tried to make sense of what had happened. "Why would Yousef want to escape?"

"Maybe he got bored sitting around in jail. I don't know. But I'm on my way to the church now to check on Ileana. No one at Little Flock is answering the phone."

Abby looked around the festival. The crowd had swollen since her arrival, and clusters of people were milling around the various displays.

"Rev. Hale and his family are probably here somewhere at the festival. Janet too. She doesn't work on Saturday, so she wasn't at church this morning when I dropped by to see Ileana."

"Did Ileana act funny, like something was going on when you saw her?"

"Not at all. She asked about Yousef, and clearly missed her husband, but that's understandable."

"I've got a man watching the ferry landing in case Yousef tries to get off the island that way. But we think he and his buddy may have left on a Scorpion racing boat that was tied up at the marina."

"A racing boat?" She shook her head and frowned. How on earth would Yousef have access to a sleek powerboat like that?

"The thing is, Bennett thinks the man who attacked him was Davor Jovanovic."

The name struck Abby like she'd been hit on the head too. "That's the name on the phony IDs we found at Oyster Inlet."

"Right. I figure the Romanian gang has gotten into the act. Either Yousef is one of them and he had help to get out of Dodge," — Henry hesitated, apparently weighing what he'd say next — "or they've kidnapped him. He's the only witness we've got who's talking and can connect the fake IDs to the counterfeiting ring in New Jersey. It may be that Yousef has become too great a liability and someone wants him eliminated before he can testify in court."

Dear God, don't let them harm Yousef.

"I'm at the church parking lot now," Henry said. "I'm going to take Ileana and her daughter into protective custody. Either Yousef is trying to flee the country, in which case he'd take his family with him. Or, if he's in danger, then so's his family."

When Abby snapped her phone closed, her mother immediately asked what was wrong.

Slowly, trying to recreate her conversation with Henry, Abby explained the situation to her mother and Rick. They appeared as dumbfounded as she was, and just as worried.

Her phone chimed again. Henry.

"Ileana and her daughter aren't here. They must have left in a hurry. All their clothes are still here, and so is their cat. I'm putting out an all points bulletin and notifying the Coast Guard." With a hurried promise to get back to her later, Henry disconnected.

As Abby explained the latest news to Rick and her mother, she felt sick to her stomach. No way would Caterina leave Comoară behind. Unless she and her mother were forced to go.

Ellen Stanton looked as helpless as Abby felt. "What can we do?"

"I don't know. But I'm absolutely sure Yousef didn't go willingly with Davor Jovanovic, or whatever his name is. He worked too hard and gave up too much getting to America in the first place to walk or run away when he was so close to achieving his goal of asylum."

Spearing his fingers through his hair, Rick appeared thoughtful. "You said Henry thinks he left in a racing boat?"

"I think he meant a boat was seen leaving the marina about that time. He didn't seem sure Yousef was onboard."

"You remember that Scorpion racing boat we saw tied up on the other side of Oyster Inlet?" Rick asked.

She thought for a moment. "Yes, I think so. White with a red stripe on it."

"You can bet it had a GPS unit onboard," he added.

Her jaw dropped open. "You think that Jovanovic was piloting that boat?"

"And maybe staying in that summer cabin, at least until he picked up his fake IDs."

"Which we managed to snatch right out from under his nose. If we'd been out there a day later —"

"The IDs would've been gone," Rick concluded.

Abby paced in front of the display table. A stranger came up and glanced through the visitor information about sights to see on the island. She ignored him.

"Rick, we have to get out to Oyster Inlet. That could be where Jovanovic has taken Yousef and his family." She handed her mother the basket Ashley had woven. "Keep this for me, please."

"You have to tell Henry what you're up to," Abby's mother warned. "You could be placing yourself in danger."

Rick grabbed for his jacket, which was hanging over the back of a folding chair. "We'll have to get back to the marina and get a boat."

"That'll take too long. Keith Gordon has his cabin cruiser moored at his dock here at the hotel. He'll let us use it, I'm sure. That'll be faster."

Over her mother's objections, Abby started off to find Keith.

"Call Henry, dear," her mother repeated.

Abby waved her agreement, but didn't stop to make the call. She'd do that once she and Rick were on the way to Oyster Inlet.

Within minutes, Abby and Rick were on-board Keith's cruiser and motoring at top speed toward the north end of Sparrow Island. The bow cut through the swells, kicking up a rooster tail of water behind the stern.

While Rick took the wheel, Abby tried to call Henry.

"Uh-oh," she said, staring at her phone.

Rick glanced over his shoulder. "What's wrong?"

"I'm not getting a signal." Cell phone coverage in the San Juan Islands was spotty at best. Apparently they were in a dead zone.

"Maybe when we're on the other side of Arrowhead Hill you'll be able to connect."

"I hope so." If they did locate Jovanovic, he could be dangerous. They'd need back up. But Abby'd had trouble with cell phone coverage near Oyster Inlet in the past. That could mean she and Rick would be on their own.

They weren't armed.

Jovanovic was. He'd pistol whipped Deputy Bennett.

The only thing they had on their side was surprise.

The shoreline sped by, an occasional cabin visible through the trees, private docks at the water's edge. In an open meadow, Abby spotted a black-tailed doe with her fawn. The doe started and fled into the shadowed safety of the forest, her offspring following close behind.

When they made the turn at the northern end of the island, the landscape changed and became more rugged. Waves battering the coastline for millennia had eroded the shore, leaving a rocky beach dotted with boulders.

Abby tried her phone again. Still no signal.

"Let's beach the boat this side of the inlet and walk in the rest of the way," Abby suggested. "If we're right and Jovanovic is there, we need to surprise him."

Rick throttled back. "Let's try the marine radio. I don't like the idea of us being a two-man, *unarmed* SWAT team unless there's no other choice."

Abby agreed. She took the wheel while Rick called the Coast Guard on the emergency frequency.

While he was explaining the situation via the radio, Abby spotted a sleek racing boat approaching from the south.

"Rick! They're here!"

She grabbed for a pair of binoculars stashed in a compartment near the wheel. Hurriedly, she adjusted the focus and scanned the open boat speeding toward the inlet. She spotted Ileana sitting in back holding Caterina in her lap. Neither of them were wearing life vests, which was foolishly unsafe at the speed the boat was flying over the water with Jovanovic at the wheel.

There was no sign of Yousef.

Holding her breath, Abby watched as the racing boat slowed marginally and turned into Oyster Inlet. If Jovanovic had noticed their boat, he'd thought nothing of it. Just another bunch of tourists on a cabin cruiser enjoying a recreational day on the water.

Rick ended his radio transmissions. "There's no Coast Guard boat in the immediate vicinity, but they're sending one now. They'll also notify Henry about what's going on."

When the racing boat was out of sight, Abby turned toward the shore. "Ileana and Caterina are on that boat with Jovanovic. I'm thinking he already brought Yousef to the cabin and then went to get the rest of the family."

"To help them all escape? Or to kill them?"

Abby swallowed hard. She didn't know. She only sensed the Lazar family was in terrible danger.

"Maybe the bunch of crooks who were smuggling him into the States demanded an additional payment after his fake IDs went missing. Kidnapping Yousef and his family might be the only way he could pay the price." That was a wild guess, but not unreasonable, given the ring of counterfeiters involved in this scheme. Greed, and protecting their own interests, was their priority. Jovanovic might have felt he had no choice.

Hurriedly, Rick started rummaging through various drawers and cupboards in the wheelhouse, then went down to the engine room. When he returned, he had a heavy crowbar with him and a flare gun.

She eyed his weapons with skepticism. They weren't exactly a match for a loaded pistol.

"Run the boat up as close to the beach as you can," he said. "I'll use the bow line to tie us off to a tree while you drop anchor."

"Got it." Easing the boat forward, she tried to slip between two large boulders that had come to rest in shallow water. She heard the boat scrape bottom. Wincing, she cut the engine. Rick splashed down over the side of the boat and she went to the stern to lower the anchor.

With the boat as secure as they could make it, she dropped into the knee-deep water, too, and scrambled up to the rocky beach. Her casual shoes and slacks weren't suited for an impromptu dip or a hike in the woods. They'd simply have to do.

The path along this side of the inlet looked seldom used. Grass grew across it. Some spots were muddy.

They'd gone only a short way when they heard voices.

Within a few more feet they spotted Ileana and her daughter still sitting in the boat at the old dock. Jovanovic towered over them, a pistol in his hand.

"If you want to see your husband alive, stay put," he ordered, before turning to walk toward the summer cabin nestled beneath the trees.

"Once he's inside, I'm going to try to get up close to the cabin without being seen," Rick whispered.

"Go ahead. If he comes back out, I'll try to distract him while you knock him over the head or something."

Rick's lips twitched with a wry smile. "Some plan, huh?" With that, he ducked behind a tree and dashed out of sight.

Abby edged forward. *Please, Lord, help and protect us and the Lazars.*

The cabin door creaked open. Yousef appeared, his hands behind his back.

"We're all going for a nice boat ride," Jovanovic said from behind him. "Thing is, the three of you won't be coming back."

Yousef struggled to get away from Jovanovic and shouted something to Ileana. She stood up in the boat, protectively standing in front of her daughter.

Picking up a rock off the ground, Abby stepped out of the shadows. "Hey, what's going on?" She tossed the stone toward Jovanovic as hard as she could. "Run, Ileana!"

The rock fell short, but her appearance was enough to momentarily startle Jovanovic. He turned the gun toward her.

Yousef used the opportunity to kick Jovanovic in the knee. He cried out as his leg buckled. Rick dashed into the scene, hitting the man's gun hand with the crowbar. The gun fell to the ground. With his foot, Yousef pushed the gun out of Jovanovic's reach. At the same time, Rick aimed his flare gun at the kidnapper.

"At this close range, this thing will blow a hole the size of a cannonball right through your middle. Don't even think about moving."

By now, Ileana had raced to her husband's side, Caterina running and crying behind her. Abby made a dash for the pistol.

Within minutes, Ileana had untied Yousef, who lifted his daughter in his arms, and Rick had used the rope to secure Jovanovic. The would-be kidnapper and illegal alien looked thoroughly dejected sitting on the ground, his back against the splintery plank wall of the cabin.

"You do not get it!" Jovanovic shouted. "I paid to come here. I have a right! You are all crooks, all of you! I did everything they told me to do. They told me I would be safe. I cannot go back. They will kill me." His last words were swallowed by a sob.

Only then did Abby realize her hands were shaking so badly she could barely hold onto the pistol. It was just as well Davor Jovanovic hadn't known how much she hated guns or the fact that she never would have been able to pull the trigger.

Taking a deep breath, she sent up a prayer of thanks that they were all safe.

It wasn't long before a Coast Guard patrol boat appeared in the inlet. They were taking Jovanovic into custody and questioning Abby and Rick when Henry arrived in his mud and dirt spattered police cruiser. He'd gotten there as fast as he could, given the road conditions.

With squealing brakes, he brought the car to a sharp stop, got out and slammed his campaign hat firmly on his head. "Is everyone okay?"

"We're fine," Abby assured him. "A little

shaken, maybe."

Giving both Abby and Rick a stern look, he shook his head. "You're also more lucky than you know that you didn't get yourselves killed. Turns out this Jovanovic character's a real killer. What did you think you were doing? Playing at cops and robbers?"

Not fooled at all by his gruff manner, Abby gave the sergeant a quick hug. "Thanks for coming to our rescue."

"Your mother and Mary would have both had my head if anything had happened to you." He *humphed* as he hugged her back. "I'm gonna talk to the Coast Guard boys, get them to release the Lazar family back to me. Then I'm gonna get a federal judge to order them released under their own recognizance, even if it is Saturday. That family's been through enough."

After a few more questions, the situation was sorted out. The Lazars climbed into Henry's police cruiser for the ride back to Green Harbor and Jovanovic was put on-board the Coast Guard patrol boat in handcuffs. He'd be detained, at least temporarily, in Bellingham.

By the time Rick and Abby returned Keith's boat to the Dorset's dock, the festival was in full swing.

It wasn't until the next day, Father's Day,

following church services that the really good news began to arrive.

Brenda Wilson, owner of the Tackle Shop, stood on a temporary stage set up especially for the Best of Sparrow Island Festival.

"We had a great Bass Fishing Classic this year," she said into a microphone. "Twenty-two father-and-son, or father-and-daughter, teams participated in the event, catching and releasing eighty-six fish."

The crowd applauded, and Abby could see Bobby McDonald and his dad standing near the stage. Crossing her fingers, she hoped they'd be the winners.

"I want to thank everyone who partici-pated," Brenda continued. "I can tell you, sport fishing is alive and well on Sparrow Island. Now . . . for the third place finish-ers." She lifted a nice sized trophy in the shape of a jumping fish and announced the father-daughter team who'd caught the third biggest fish in the contest.

The second place trophy was slightly larger. Bobby began to squirm next to his father and then gave a little jump when their names were *not* called.

When, at last, Brenda held up the win-ning trophy — a good two feet tall — Bobby looked like he was about to come out of his skin. *Me too,* Abby thought, laughing to herself.

"I'm proud to announce the first place prize for catching a three-pound six-ounce sea bass goes to . . . Neil and Bobby Mc-Donald of Green Harbor."

Everyone hooted and hollered, including Abby.

"You look happy about the winner," a male voice said behind her.

Startled, she turned to find Mel Reeves looking down at her with his kind, intelligent eyes. "You came!" Pleasure shot through her.

"I had a personal invitation." Reaching back, he drew an attractive, dark-haired woman forward. She looked to be in her midforties and had a figure that would be the envy of a twenty-year-old. "I brought a friend. Megan Moore accompanies me on my geocaching sojourns when she's not selling real estate. Meet Abby Stanton."

After a brief moment of regaining her mental equilibrium, Abby extended her hand. "Welcome to the Best of Sparrow Island."

With a practiced smile, Megan said, "Thank you. Mel was quite taken with you, Abby, and couldn't stay away. He was anxious that we meet."

"I'm glad he brought you along." More self-conscious than she'd care to admit, Abby glanced around. "Let me introduce you to some of the other geocachers who've shown up for the event. We've had more than twenty active cachers drop by our information table, including some from the mainland who came for the day, plus those who've been asking questions about the hobby."

"The more the merrier, I always say." Megan tucked her arm through Mel's and smiled up at him.

Suppressing a laugh, mostly at her own foolish thoughts, Abby led the couple to Rick and their geocaching table. After she made the introductions, she eased away. She wanted to congratulate Bobby for his winning trophy.

When she reached him, he was clutching the trophy and grinning like crazy as Sandy took a picture of him and his father.

"Good job!" Abby said when the two of them were free to move again. She slapped Bobby's hand in a high-five.

"This is the biggest, best trophy I've ever got!"

"Not that his room isn't already filled with assorted trophies," Sandy commented with a smile of her own. "Pretty soon we'll have to build a separate trophy room onto the house just to hold them all."

"Yeah! That'd be neat." Bobby's grin grew ever wider.

A flock of his friends surrounded Bobby wanting to congratulate him and touch the trophy.

In contrast to Bobby, Neil looked more relieved than proud. "We got skunked so many times, I was afraid I'd have to buy a fish at the Green Grocer and hang it on his hook. That son of mine is one competitive kid."

Abby laughed. "He also loves to spend time with his dad, in case you hadn't noticed."

The corners of his lips kicked up into a smile. "Yeah, pretty neat, isn't it?" he said, echoing his son's youthful vocabulary.

As she left the McDonalds to enjoy their celebration, she noticed Henry Cobb, Agent Burns and the entire Lazar family walking across the festival grounds. She hurried toward them.

"It's so good to see you here," she said to Ileana. "Is everything all right?"

"More than all right." She took Yousef's hand and held on tight. Her free arm was hooked around Caterina as though to keep her safe from harm.

Grinning from ear-to-ear, Henry held up a sheet of official-looking paper. "Agent Burns brought this over from the mainland himself. It's an order from an Undersecretary of State giving Yousef and Ileana, and their daughter, political asylum in the United States. After a year, they'll be eligible to apply for citizenship."

Stunned, Abby checked with Burns for confirmation. "My boss, Hugo Baron, spoke with a friend at the State Department about the Lazar situation. Could that have helped?"

"Probably didn't hurt. But the fact is, the State Department, as well as Immigration and Customs, has been after that ring of counterfeiters for several years. Based on Yousef's statements, they've already rounded up several of the ringleaders. With his testimony, we'll be able to put them away for a long time. And that includes Jovanovic, who claims he was acting on their orders to get rid of Yousef and his family. It was the only way they'd let him *earn* a new set of forged documents."

"Congratulations!" Unable to help herself, she hugged Ileana and then Yousef, who blushed a bright red.

"It is you and your sister, and Sergeant Cobb as well as Agent Burns, of course, who we have to thank for this," Yousef said. "We are most grateful."

God might have had a part in it too, Abby thought with a smile.

"Where is Mary?" Ileana asked.

"Probably at the booth where she's selling the merchandise from her knitting group. And your lovely decorative rocks."

They all went in search of Mary to give her the good news. They found her talking with Keith Gordon.

After a suitable number of hugs and a few tears, Mary said, "Keith, if you haven't already hired a new pastry chef, I think Yousef would like to apply for the job."

Yousef straightened. "I would be very pleased if you would consider me for a position, sir."

Keith glanced over his shoulder toward the fish fry area the cooks had set up and were getting underway. The scent of fish sizzling in hot oil had started to infiltrate the fresh ocean air.

"You know what, Yousef? I'm short one fry cook right now. How about filling in starting this afternoon and we'll worry about the paperwork later. From what I've read, I think you'll be an excellent addition to the Dorset staff."

Yousef was so quick to agree, he nearly

choked trying to find the right words. Meanwhile, Ileana started to cry from sheer happiness.

Abby felt emotion clog her throat too.

Later, as she and her friends sat around a picnic table after their fish dinner, Abby watched Yousef talking with his new co-workers and their customers. He looked perfectly at ease. At home.

In the cooling evening air, with the scattering of clouds in the western sky turning a light pink, she recalled God's promise to David in the Bible. "And I will provide a place for my people Israel and will plant them so that they can have a home of their own and no longer be disturbed. Wicked people will not oppress them anymore, as they did at the beginning. . . . The Lord himself will establish a house for you" (2 Samuel 7:10–11).

She chuckled to herself. Not only had the Lazar family found a place for themselves, Ashley Tomlins was finding her way to her Native American roots too. Even Miss Mischief, aka Comoară, had found a new home.

And that's exactly what the Lord had intended.

ABOUT THE AUTHOR

Charlotte Carter has authored more than forty novels and many nonfiction books. She has received various awards, including the prestigious National Reader's Choice Award and the Career Achievement Award by the *Romantic Times* magazine. Charlotte and her husband live in Southern California, and have two daughters and five grandchildren.